PHANTASY - LAND OF THE BEYOND

BOOK 1:

PHANTASY - LAND OF THE BEYOND

JUST DAVE

PARTRIDGE

A Penguin Random House Company

To order additional copies of this book, contact
Toll Free 800 101 2657 (Singapore)
Toll Free 1 800 81 7340 (Malaysia)
orders.singapore@partridgepublishing.com

www.partridgepublishing.com/singapore

CONTENTS

This book is
Dedicated to
HE who got me started in the first place when I was lost for my entire life until now, my parents for without them I wouldn't be here in the first place and a very special friend of mine in my heart whom the character "Snowpetal" was based on.

"I vow with my life everything in this book is borne of my very own imagination and no one else's!"

_D-Man

Author's Note:

P lease be forewarned that this is a book of modern-day fairy-tale fantasy fiction unlike most others of its kind. This is also the very first time I have put in so much effort and time writing my first novel. I hope you readers enjoy reading it as much as I enjoyed creating it.

I first started writing this book back in 2009 which was a truly bad year for me as I was jobless that whole year so I had lots of time to burn which made me start writing. But I stopped in 2010 and decided to take a break simply because I finally found a job as a security officer then and was probably too busy working and too lazy to continue writing.

Between the periods of 2011-2013 I did try to continue with this book but somehow lost the interest and will to carry on with it. Initially, when I had just started work on this novel, I had thought to complete it by the year 2011 and get it published somehow by the year 2012 simply because it would coincide with the years found in my prologue. Unfortunately, there were quite a few factors I had to take into consideration before I could do that.

First of all, I was brand new to the world of writing (as a career) and knew no publisher or anyone associated with one even though I had worked in one of the major bookstores in Singapore before (Popular Bookstore). Second thing was the fact that I had lost my link to my book as I had not touched it for more than one year since

2010. No, it's not writer's block or anything like that really. I could still continue writing but it wouldn't be the same anymore. It would end up a totally different book and not what I had in mind in the first place. And thirdly, the power box of the desk top I had saved my work that I had worked very hard on up to that point broke down back in 2011 and I lost everything...

It wasn't till 2012, a year later that I was able get a new pc but even with a new computer, there was nothing I could do as it meant I had to start all over again with my book and I couldn't. It wouldn't be the same book and story as I had initially imagined and planned. Then I remembered that I had saved all the documents from my old pc to an external hard disk drive before it broke down including my uncompleted novel which, for some reason, did not function as well! I panicked! But I didn't know what to do then. Was this the end of my first novel? And so I forgot about the book I had planned to write and published.

Reality has a strange and funny way of getting things done. In 2013 I knew this guy who was, to me, pretty knowledgeable about IT and computers. In fact, I had known him for more than half a year and it never crossed my mind to ask him if he could help me fix my broken external hard disk drive until someone else I knew asked if I or anyone I knew could help her fix a memory card she had trouble storing data into. I immediately thought of my "IT" friend.

Long story short, I eventually managed to savage what was left of my old HDD and continued writing my novel. Thing now was, my job as an export administrator was always keeping me busy from finding time for anything else. I was actually procrastinating with the completion of my first novel which by this time had become part of a trilogy.

Something dramatic and drastic happened to me on the third of April, 2014, that changed my life forever. Most people may consider this a bad sign but to me, it's a blessing in disguise! Yup, I suffered my first major heart attack at the age of 41! After a series of tests, it was discovered that all the arteries of my heart were blocked, especially the main artery which was entirely blocked and even a heart by-pass could only clear at the most, fifty percent. It was a very serious case, so serious in fact that my heart operation was scheduled on the tenth of April, 2014, barely a week after I was admitted to hospital, which was my very first time staying in one, or two, as was my case and I know in my heart it won't be my last either.

I was discharged on the fifteen of April, 2014, just five days after my by-pass and was given three months medical leave by my heart surgeon, one of the best in Singapore, if not the best (in my own opinion). Well, what was I to do with three months' worth of strictly staying at home with nothing else to do but rest and recover from the wound on my chest and that big scar left behind which I am so proud of? Why, I decided to continue with my novel persevering to the end and making sure it got published and read! But before I could get it published I had to find a publisher and that's when I finally decided to contact *this* publisher via email I had come across by accident one day about a year ago surfing the internet while bored with nothing better to do...

And the rest is history.

By the way, when I come to think about it carefully, it seems as if I was meant to create this book of mine whether I like it or not. The circumstances leading to me first coming up with the concept, searching for the right publisher (by accident?) to finally finding time and energy to complete it wasn't merely a huge chain of coincidences. There is definitely an unseen force at work here in my life and I believe in it! Do you?

The next few paragraphs are actually the original author's note which I have kept untouched. Read them before reading the rest of my novel including the prologue and epilogue. You'll be surprised.

It has always been my staunch belief that within each and every one of us, no matter who we think we are or where we come from, there is at least one story we would like to tell and share with everyone else.

Captured in this very first novel of yours truly is the essence of such a tale. Now, I feel the time is right to open up and share this (so-called) fantasy story of mine with the rest of the world. Although this book is purely just a fabrication of ridiculous imagination, tall-tales and far-fetched thinking, it is also undeniably based (partially) on certain facts and true events. Not surprisingly though, some of the characters in this book were based on real-life encounters and what few friends I have.

Anyway, it has been one of my lifelong dreams to write at least one book and make it known to the entire world before my demise. So here it is! I bade a most warm welcome to the purely mad and totally twisted and unpredictable world of yours truly; D-Man, the Story-Teller. Carry on if you dare, for what comes after is... Well, I hope I have aroused your curiosity enough to a degree that you, the reader, would want to continue reading. But before you begin exploring the rest of this novel, do bear in mind that every journey and path begin from a certain point and that starting point has always been from the individual that makes all of us so unique and different from one other; us ourselves. Enjoy while you still can... You have been warned after all...

PROLOGUE:

THE BEGINNING OF AN END, PART 1.

(Warning: This is not a science-fiction novel you, the reader, are about to read even though the prologue is set in the distant future. There is a reason for this and it can be found in Book 3, the last part of this trilogy. But for now...)

In the Earth year of 2122, life as we now know has been drastically altered. As a matter of fact, everything changed the day Mother Gaia or planet Earth as it was more commonly known, was completely and utterly, destroyed, a decade ago. By then, most of the Earthlings had already departed in spaceships by the horde to either live on other planets specially tailored to provide the same living conditions as the original Earth, or to simply drift aimlessly around the vast Universe in their own special autonomous spaceships known as 'Floaters'.

There were only a handful of such floaters even though the technology by then had become vastly superior compared to that of the modern era. Main reason was that the materials needed to build such massive space vessels capable of sustaining life for generations to come had grown scarce and whatever was found and used to construct them eventually depleted what remained of Earth's natural resources. Because of that, each floater cost billions of dollars to build and not many people had that kind of money. In fact, some floaters even housed more than 2 different families which eventually, over the light years, merged as one.

Sadly, one of the main reasons for the demise of our beloved Earth can be found in the above-mentioned paragraph. But there were *other* crucial factors involved. Frankly-speaking, it all boiled down to the top predator on earth as the one and *only* cause for the ultimate destruction of the only place in this entire galaxy that has been home to our kind for far longer than we can remember – us, human beings!

As mentioned earlier, some of the floaters contained two or more different families and the Star Bright was one such floater. Like all unique floaters that were home to more than one family, it was really colossal and impressive, about twice the size of a normal floater and approximately the magnitude of a city or small island.

It was bedtime for the youngest denizens of one such magnificent floater, Star Bright. Nettle, Sukie and Zukie were already cozily tucked into their soft warm individual beds by their caretaker robots. Without fail, their portly great-grandfather appeared on the wall-mounted standard 60-inch television screens of their respective bedrooms half an hour before their bedtime, all smiles and ready for their nightly story-time conference before they wandered off to dreamy slumber-land.

Old Dave was his usual jovial and confident self when his three favorite and youngest great-grand-children greeted him. He had other great-grand-children but they were all a lot older and away on holiday on some foreign planets galaxies away having the time of their life (teenagers, they never change, not in a million gazillion light tears!). Nettle, Sukie and Zukie were all too young to travel out of the safety zone of their floater but they didn't mind that since they knew they would all grow up in due time like the rest of their siblings and cousins, ready to take on the unknown boundaries of the mysterious immense dark vacuum known as Deep Space. But for now, they were contented just to lie in bed waiting patiently for another of their great-grandfather's ancient fairy tales.

"So what's on the menu tonight, Great Grand-Dada?" six year-old Sukie, with her big innocent and curious hazel-brown eyes, raised her left eyebrow in anticipation at her great-grandfather.

"Wait, didn't you mention that you're fresh out of bedtime stories to tell us the other night?", quipped the ever smarter-than-your-average-kid Zukie, also six and the identical twin of Sukie but who already was starting to think and act like a grown-up.

"Well, I...," trailed their rather stunned grandfather who was indeed caught by surprise by the clever remark for he had long forgotten what he had said the night before. Old age must finally be catching up with Dave for he was already 150 years old (it seemed space-age technology did indeed allow people to live longer than the expected natural life span, *but at what cost?*).

"Don't worry about those two little ones, Great Grand-Dada. I know you didn't mean what you said the other night," it was the cool-headed and sensible ten year old Nettle who saved their great-grandfather from further embarrassment as usual.

But old Dave's face was already flushed when he said that he had meant what he said the other night about running out of bedtime stories to tell his three favorite great-grand-children. The look of disbelief on the three kids' faces was enough to put the smile back on his face.

"Actually, he-he (sheepish grin), I'm saving the best for the last but since you kids insist... I guess I have no choice but to tell you kids this amazing but true tale that *did* happen in a distant land and time much unlike ours."

And so, without much further ado, here begins the actual story....

(This concludes the Prologue.)

CHAPTER 1:

THE BEGINNING OF AN END, PART 2.

Seated squarely in the middle of the eternally peaceful and evergreen kingdom of *Phantasy* (pronounced *Fee-yond-derr-see*), known also as the Land of the Beyond, was the fortified and mighty castle where the old and dying King Otellus and his two young sons, Prince Devonus and Prince Secondras lived, together with all 108 of their faithful servants.

The kingdom of *Phantasy* itself was pretty much an isolated country surrounded by nothing but the vast ocean as far as the naked eye can see and hundreds of tiny, wild and mostly unexplored and uninhabited islands waiting to be discovered. Not much of its existence was known to the outside world and vice versa. Nonetheless, it was a contented and peaceful country since everything its denizens required could be found on the land itself. Everyday was a dreamy and happy affair for the people living in *Phantasy* as they went about their daily lives without the slightest hint or notion of worries and troubles.

Yet the Land of the Beyond was as mysterious as it was far away and very much beyond the reach of the rest of the world. Not much of its past was known and it did not ever cross the minds of the common folks living in the sleepy kingdom itself to ever query. Indeed, for the inhabitants of the kingdom of *Phantasy*, it was like a dream come true. How it started and when it would end didn't really matter. For ignorance was bliss. And blissful times was all that mattered at the moment, especially for the sovereignty of *Phantasy*. However, the multifarious of ancient ruins scattered all across the kingdom itself was a testimony to the present peaceful kingdom's chaotic and dark past. Perhaps it wasn't such a good idea to ignore the signs of war and rampage from past eras after all...

It was another hot lazy afternoon and the sun was already far to the west when the aged and wise king decided to send for the elder of his two sons, Prince Devonus, who was also the stronger and more sensible among them, to have a private word with him. Prince Secondras, on the other hand, was the 'fairer' and weaker of the two, always pale and sickly and a disappointment and failure in the eyes of his father. He was also considered a bane to King Otellus since Queen Maya, his mother, whom his father, the king, had loved dearly, died almost immediately after giving birth to him. And because of that, the two hardly met or talked. But because the king was a man with a golden heart as all great kings should have, he had allowed the younger prince to continue staying at the castle, living his princely but otherwise useless life.

"My child, do you know why I summoned you?" gasped King Otellus.

The two were alone in the king's private chamber (or so they thought) and the young prince reflected hard and long before he finally opened his mouth. "No, not really, Sire. But I guess it must be something really big and important since my ears are the only ears privileged enough for whatever secrets you have to depart to me." As usual, Prince Devonus had his way with words (especially among the ladies) which never failed to bring out the smiles and giggles.

A weak smile formed on the wrinkled face of the older man as he said softly, "My time in this world is almost at an end. My son, I have always considered you to be my only child and rightful heir to my throne. It is almost time to fulfill that part of the prophecy and for me to move on and join your mother in the next world."

"Wait father! Are you saying...? But, what about Secondras? He's my brother and your son too! True, our beloved mother died soon after he was born but it's not fair to put the blame on him! Secondras has been feeling guilty all his life and he's only 17! Besides, he's been ill with a strange disease that has puzzled every single physician throughout the entire kingdom ever since he was two. Isn't that punishment enough for him?!!"

Somewhere in the hidden adjoining room built for such a purpose of spying and eavesdropping on the king's activities in his private room, someone was indeed listening intently to the secret dialogue between King Otellus and Prince Devonus. A young, pale and slender figure with shoulder-length flowing auburn hair and the most alluring pair of deep green eyes was trying his best to catch every word said between father and son. A smile formed at the side of his mouth when he heard his elder brother siding him. Indeed, Prince Secondras wasn't that dense and feeble as everybody had imagined him to be. Oh no, au contraire, he just made himself appear that way so nobody would suspect him for what he had been planning all along – vengeance!

Prince Devonus was getting emotional with each passing second and King Otellus thought the elder prince had lost his head but he was too tired to do more. "Calm down my son! There is more than meets the eye here. Now compose yourself as a prince should and listen to me. And hearken well!" whizzed the old and exhausted king.

The young prince's breathing was starting to return to normal as he stared at his father, albeit with a rather odd gazed look on his face, a shrunken husk of the proud and majestic commanding figure of the king he once was, no doubt. But he was still king nonetheless. There was a twinkle in Prince Devonus's eyes who was once again his usual relaxed self as he waited patiently now for his father, the king to catch his breath and continue with whatever was on his mind.

"Many years before I met your mother, God bless her soul in heaven, and had you and that cursed brother of yours as a result of our most beautiful unions, I had an encounter with this ancient and mysterious figure of a hooded-robe man who imparted many incredible tales, all from unheard-of lands beyond ours. And at the end of his spectacular tales, he had this prophecy for me."

There was a long pause. The old king's eyes had this undeniable faraway dreamy look as memories from his young days came flooding back.

"I was but a young man then, younger than you are now, my child. But unlike you, I was full of energy and impulsive, forever ready and impatient to set out and see the world for myself! It was the last day of my early adventures as the Crown Prince of *Phantasy*. I had just turned 21 and was eager to perform my duties as the next ruler of our kingdom. Hah-hah, it was more like I couldn't wait to be king just to show off!"

The king coughed and there was blood. Prince Devonus panicked but King Otellus, with a weak gesture of his right hand said there was nothing anyone could do about his weakened condition. He was a man who had grown wise with each passing year. One thing he had learned over the years was never to fight the inevitable. When it's time to go, just let go. No point holding on to what's not there anymore. Nothing in this world was permanent and he found that out the hard way when his beloved wife had passed away after the birth of their second child. The love between King Otellus and Queen Maya was stronger than any bond forged between two sentient beings but even that did not last forever.

With a weary sigh, the king continued with his story.

"It was the glorious day I was to be crowned king. We have come from a long line of having only a single child born every generation in our royal family and that child is always male. There is even a legend behind this tradition as I was told by my father as a child. I know not how true it is. But I have been feeling bad ever since that legacy had been broken by yours truly. Maybe that's why so many unexpected bad things have happened over the years...," and tears welled in the old king's sad eyes (think along the line of the *arranged death* of Queen Maya).

"Anyway, moments after I was crowned king, there emerged news that a certain famous soothsayer from a faraway land was passing by ours. His predictions were always accurate, so they said. Young and curious as I was then, never thinking of the consequences of my actions, I quickly sent for this enigma of a seer. All I merely wanted was to have some fun with him since I had never believed in any of that sorcery magic stuff. To me it was all a hoax and nothing more than child's play trickery. It was also the first thing I wanted to do as king - to prove to my loyal subjects that there was no such thing as predictions of the future, much less true and precise ones!"

"But... I was soon proven wrong. When he finally appeared before me after some searching by the royal guards, something about his... presence intrigued yet repulsed me at the same time. Although covered fully from head to toe by a hooded robe, there emanated a very foreign yet mesmerizing aura about him. When I mentioned that it was disrespectful of him not to remove the hood that covered his face in the presence of a king, he simply claimed that a curse would befall my kingdom should he do so. His comments very much surprised and angered me but queerly, those heated emotions lasted only but a short while."

"Before long, he did pull the hood behind his head as ordered by me and what caught my eyes were those disturbing yet enchanting deep green eyes of his..."

At this point, King Otellus's half closed eyes widened with terror as he realized something.

"Wait... Isn't the color of Secondras's eyes...emerald?" The king was trembling at this point as his body turned cold with fear.

Prince Devonus said nothing as he placed more blankets on his dying father's shivering frail body.

"I think you have said enough for today and should get some rest, father dearest," Prince Devonus turned away from the king with a deeply perplex look on his face. It was already late in the evening and the sun had long ago set in the west.

Dinner that night was a brief and silent affair and everyone retired early for the night.

The entire kingdom was in a complete state of grief the next day as King Otellus was found cold and lifeless that morning on his death-bed. What made matters worse was that the younger prince had disappeared that same day. It was rumored that Prince Secondras was so heart-broken by the death of his beloved father and his conscience so plagued by the guilt that was building up over the years that he had caused the untimely death of his mother, he had totally lost his mind that morning by the news of the unexpected death of his father and thus escaped to who-knows-where as a result. Unfortunately, the truth was nothing even remotely close.

Sadly enough, the one hit hardest by the old king's death was none other than his elder (and only) son, Prince Devonus. He kept himself to his room for many weeks after the old king's passing, pondering over his father's last words as the rest of the castle searched day and night without rest for the missing prince. But Prince Secondras was never found. Eventually, as the weeks grew into months and the months grew into years, he was given up for dead. The most popular belief was that he had silently sneaked out of the castle when everybody else was grieving at the loss of King Otellus that morning, went into the wild forests that surrounded the castle and was devoured by one of the wild beasts that inhibited them.

Well, life had to go on, missing prince or not. Three years had passed since the demise of King Otellus and the unexplained disappearance of Prince Secondras. Meanwhile, Prince Devonus had just turned 21. He still had not solved the mystery of his father's last words. But there were more important things on his mind now. He had just reached adulthood after all and it was the kingdom of

Phantasy's tradition to crown the grown-up prince king at that age. Prince Devonus was in a state of ecstasy and other mixed emotions during his inauguration as the King of *Phantasy*. The day he had waited for had finally arrived and he was considered a child no more.

Those of royalty and great importance had gathered at the grand courtroom where the king held all his audiences with everybody who's anybody or nobody who had problems, people from the common folks to nobles, the filthy rich, the famous and those of royal blood like the king himself. King Devonus had just been freshly crowned and everybody was as happy as could be. There were the usual singing and dancing and feasting and drinking and clowning about by the royal jesters.

Everybody who was anybody was in such a merry-making mood and nobody was permitted to exhibit any negative emotions. It was officially a holiday as well and laughter could be heard throughout the entire kingdom. King Devonus was seated on his golden throne and joining in the celebration, talking and cracking jokes with his loyal subjects when all eyes were suddenly drawn to this mysterious robed figure who had entered the courtroom most noiselessly and without anybody noticing, not even the ever vigil royal guards who had kept a straight face despite the merry-making that was going on around them. All the singing and dancing and silly and playful antics had stopped and there was only silence as everybody stared doubtfully at this singular intruder.

"Hello stranger, whoever you are, please have a seat and help yourself to the refreshments," King Devonus greeted the robed figure who was hiding his face under a hood, ever the gracious host. Something was amiss about the hooded-robe man. He seemed oddly familiar to King Devonus yet he couldn't quite put his finger on it.

It wasn't until he had exposed his head for all to see that everyone present gasped in shock and King Devonus recognized the mysterious figure at once. He stood up and nearly choked on his own words as old memories that he had purposely pushed to the most inner parts of his brain came flooding out again.

"Secondras? My dearest long-lost brother...is that really you standing in front of me?!!" the young king fought back tears of joy as he recognized the shoulder-length auburn hair, thin lips, high cheekbones and disturbingly deep green eyes of the younger brother he thought he had lost for good.

Deep green eyes... Something about his brother's deep green eyes caused King Devonus to put on his guard. Then he remembered his late father's last words. And he remembered the story about the hooded-robe figure that had appeared when his father was crowned king and the many wondrous tales of other magical faraway lands beyond their kingdom. He had deep green eyes. But no, that was a long time ago and King Otellus had mentioned that that man was old, almost ancient in fact, with long flowing hair and beard the color of snow.

As if he knew what was going on through the mind of the young king, which he probably did, the man whom King Devonus had referred to as Secondras uttered, "Yes, it is indeed I, Secondras. But I am neither your brother nor a prince, your Majesty."

To the shock and horror of all those present in the courtroom that fateful day, Secondras started to go through a major transformation. His youthful and smooth skin turned old and wrinkled, he grew thinner and appeared haggard, a beard started to sprout from his once clean-shaven chin and his hair grew longer and turned white, as did his beard. But those deep green eyes, they remained dark emerald, flashing with a pure madness and evil no one had ever witnessed before.

Being the smart man that he had always been, King Devonus had by then realized that he had always been an only child as was the custom of their kingdom. His younger brother had merely been an illusion. A multitude of questions were running through the young king's head as he absorbed the events that were unfolding before his very eyes.

"Why? Why, why, *WHY*!!!"

With a bow, "Allow me to formally introduce myself, Sire. My name is indeed Secondras but I'm no prince, let alone am your younger brother. I am instead and indeed, a warlock, and a most powerful one too I might add. I control hordes of destructive demons that never fail to do my evil biding. I can also take on the form of anything and anyone I desire! I can even control minds if I want to." (What, so now he's bragging...son-of-a-demon that he is!)

"Perhaps you may have heard of me? I was the one who singlehanded destroyed half the kingdom many, many decades ago. Oh, that's right, you weren't even born yet!" Secondras was basking in the attention he was receiving from every pair of eyes now staring at him. He had become the center of attention, no more the new king.

Secondras the Warlock was most defiant with his head held high as once again he assumed the form of the young Prince Secondras that everyone was once so familiar with, especially King Devonus, who could only watch with his eyes wide open, feeling helpless, too numb now to do or say anything.

"Actually, I'm here today to deliver the prophecy that's rightfully yours. You know, the one your father failed to reveal to you before he died?" and Secondras winked slyly at the king who was never his brother.

"He was a good man who ruled his kingdom fairly and wisely, King Otellus. His part of the prophecy had been fulfilled. So now it's your turn, or rather, your future son's who is yet to be born."

"Mark my words, King Devonus, for the son who shall be born to you nine years from now WILL BE THE DOWNFALL OF YOUR KINGDOM!!!"

Having accomplished the task that he had come to carry out, Secondras the Warlock vanished in style in a cloud of thick black smoke, leaving everyone speechless, their hair disarrayed and their faces drained of all blood.

Then quite unexpectedly, Secondras's voice was heard but himself not seen. "Oh, and did I forget to mention that the child's mother will lose a lot of blood during his birth and thus die as a result? MUAHAHAHA!!!..." That eerie evil laughter was the last that anyone had heard of Secondras the Warlock, or so they thought.

By this time though, the damage had been done. For the second part of the prophecy had been delivered and would be fulfilled sooner or later, just as the first had been. (And only God knows how many parts to that prophecy there were altogether!)

King Devonus was a changed man overnight. From a cheerful, gregarious and patient man who was always ready to lend a helping hand and ear even when he was still a prince, the young king had become a shadow of his former self. He kept to himself mostly, locked behind his kingly private chamber and hardly talked to anyone anymore. He still held his daily audiences with his loyal subjects, although with a sad and somewhat distracted face. But he did not allow any women or even girls to attend them and the only female he allowed close to him then was his aged nanny. He had love and respect for her but it was nothing in any way romantic of course.

For many years after the second portion of the prophecy was delivered, King Devonus kept away from all female company and presence as best as he could. As time passed by though, he gradually forgot about the cursed prediction and eventually returned to the jovial and sensible man that he once was. At the ripe age of twenty-eight, the young king met and fell madly in love with the loveliest lass he had chanced upon during one of his hunting trips in the wild forests. Her name was Katrina and she turned out to be one of the (favorite) granddaughters of King Devonus's personal nanny. They were married after a brief one year courtship. Not many people approved of their marriage for Katrina was a commoner after all, even though she had come from a rich family and her father was an influential merchant who had traveled far and wide, even beyond the Land of the Beyond.

Sadly, history has a funny, if not tragic, way of repeating itself. It was only natural that Queen Katrina was pregnant not long after the new royal couple was married. And as her belly grew bigger week after week and month after month, the evil laughter and last words of Secondras the Warlock resonated in King Devonus's head. He had grown wiser and hence more patient now. But he was still just a man like everyone else within, king or no king. There were certain things even a man of such a powerful status could not prevent and the prophecy was but one of them.

King Devonus prayed hard as the birth of his newborn son drew nearer and nearer. But alas, the day the new baby boy was born, Queen Katrina had lost too much blood due to the rupture of one of her ovaries and died a most agonizing and painful death not long after the new Crown Prince was delivered.

Once again, King Devonus had become a changed man. Only this time, the effect was much, much more devastating and permanent. He was a truly heartbroken man now and he could not bear to cast even one tiny glance in the direction of his newborn son at all. Every time he tried, he was reminded of the fate of his beloved and now, very dead wife Queen Katrina, and the prophecy that had come true for him just as it did for his father, the late King Otellus.

It was at this time that Secondras the Warlock appeared before the broken king who had wished with the remaining pieces of his broken heart that he too, was among the dead.

"Well, hello, hello, so we meet again, my dear King Devonus." The warlock was in his true form this time, old and haggard yet dangerously potent nonetheless. And his face was all twisted with a wicked toothless grin that looked like it could never be wiped off. He had chosen to come before the sad and heartbroken king when he was all alone, in his private chamber, just hours after the birth of his son and death of his wife. Secondras knew this was the best time to strike for the grieving king was at his most vulnerable then.

"I need to have a private word with you, your Majesty. And no time is better than here and now, muahahaha!" The grotesquely distorted grin on Secondras's face appeared even wider as he carried on.

Normally, any man would have fainted at the sight of the real Secondras but no, not our King Devonus. He had become an indifferent man altogether, one who had lost all interest in life ever since his beloved Queen Katrina passed away. He also understood now the anguish and pain his late father, King Otellus had felt then at the loss of their beloved Queen Maya. In other words, King Devonus was now a man with a heart of stone, devoid of most feelings, saved for the intense hatred and loathe he felt for his newborn child. Although he had just gained a heir to his throne, he had also just lost the one woman he loved the most and being the hopelessly romantic man that he was, the king would have gladly sacrificed his newborn son for the return of his dead wife, even if for no more than an hour or so. Which King Devonus, in a moment of utmost folly, did, and regretted later.

"What do you want from me now?" questioned King Devonus as he stared Secondras the hideous Warlock straight in the face.

With that smug sneer and usual mad look and sparkle in his eyes, Secondras simply shrugged and hissed, "Well, you know what my heartless heart desires, my king. Tell you what... I'll prove I'm not the evildoer of a warlock that I truly am by bringing your dead Katrina back to life if you will let me have the new crown prince, yesssss." It was a demand and not a request the warlock had just stated.

King Devonus, though now a grief-stricken man mourning the loss of his dearest departed wife, kept his cool about him still and was no fool. He knew this proposition was simply too good to be true. However, the temptation was too much to resist and after a short hesitation nodded his head. "Alright, have it your way then."

"Very well then, Sire. I'll see to the preparations and be back in a few days for my...deliciously tender prize, muahahaha," and thus, rubbing his crooked hands in glee and with a puff of black smoke, Secondras the Warlock exited the castle. Or did he? (I don't know, why not ask him yourself.)

Love...is pretty much a double-edged sword. It cuts both ways and can be such a powerful and sometimes, dangerous, emotion. It can make or break any man and whole kingdoms even! Look what it did to our poor King Devonus. He had always ruled with a clear head and open heart, with no room for mistakes. He never mixed work with his personal life. Yet look at him now, all sad and alone in his ridiculously spacious bedroom (which was approximately twice the size of a standard 5-room HDB flat in today's Singapore), with his *un*dead wife seated at an awkward position on their king-sized luxury waterbed, staring blanking at nothing...

"Katrina! Is that really you?!!" King Devonus was truly overjoyed at the sight of his wife as fresh hot streams of tears rolled over his grunt handsome cheeks (yes, he had been crying alone in his private chambers even long before the evil and perverted warlock paid him a visit). A fierce battle was now being fought inside him as his heart was telling him "Yes!" but his head was telling him "No, silly, that's not your wife, she is *dead*!"

As he walked over and hugged her, King Devonus could only smell death and decay and the unusually strong stench of dried blood instead of the usual favorite tropical fruity perfume his wife was so fond of wearing, when she was still alive, that is. She looked at him with black and dull gazed eyes instead of the passionate almond-shaped dark brown eyes that he had grown so accustomed to. Her body was icy cold and stiff too, not at all like the usual warm and soft curves of the Katrina he knew so intimately.

"Katrina?" asked the king. "What happened to you?" (Isn't it obvious, you love-smitten king! You're talking to a zomb... Oh, never mind, what's the point?)

His wife was still in her white birth gown with the lower part covered in dark dried blood, *her* dried blood. She turned her head slowly and mechanically and after a long pause, as if she had forgotten how to speak, finally spoke in a low growl that Devonus did not recognize as Katrina's once sweet and soothingly melodious voice. "My lord...is that you? Where am I? It was so...dark and cold there..."

"Hush, my dearest, rest for you're still weak from the blood lost..." King Devonus's voice trailed off for he could not bear to even speak of their newborn son, crown prince or not. Despite his clearly deceased wife's undead appearance and demonic-quality voice, the romantic king treated her as if she was still alive and well. But all was not well. The appearance of his dead wife cast more doubts and worries in Devonus's already troubled mind. He made his wife who had just returned from the land of the dead (zombie, zombie, ahhhh!) lie down on their king-sized waterbed, and sleep. (Seriously, aren't the dead *already* 'asleep'???)

But in his mind the young king knew that was not possible. That was when he decided to get out of his room for some fresh air. King Devonus locked the thick and heavy double doors made of the sturdiest oak behind him, giving strict instructions to the two beefy royal guards standing outside never to rush in and do anything should they even hear the slightest noise coming from within. It was more for their own safety than anything else.

The cool evening breeze blowing across his handsome yet sorrowful face was just what King Devonus needed to clear his heavy heart and puzzled mind. Standing in the royal garden staring into the late afternoon sky, the young troubled king was enveloped by exotic fruit trees, plants and beautiful singing birds of every color imaginable. But it was not the picturesque scenery and soothing environment that he had come for. He had come to the open garden to clear his head and the cool early evening breeze and song-like chirping from the birds were working their magic on the troubled young king. He had just started to relax and soak in the cooling and calm atmosphere when a surprisingly womanly shrill cry followed by "No! Stay back, stay away from me! Please!" and more (manly) screams shattered the serene evening air.

King Devonus was sure it was coming from the direction of his royal bedroom where he had left his (undead) Katrina to rest. By the time he got there, the two heavy wooden doors had been flung wide opened with such an unearthly ferocity that they hung limply at awkward angles by their sides, their hinges exposed and broken. The two royal guards supposedly guarding his royal bedroom were nowhere to be seen. King Devonus rushed in to an empty bedroom. His waterbed was a mess and the floor wet from the water leaking from the ruptures. A most foul stench which strangely reminded the king of graveyards and death lingered in the air. Otherwise, everything else remained the same before he had left the room. Everything except the fact that his, well, zombified wife was missing!

A disembodied voice was suddenly heard in the king's bedroom saying, "I hope you enjoyed the short rendezvous you had with your dead wife, your Majesty. Oh, why the sad and resigned look? Didn't you know that the spell I cast on your dead Katrina lasts for no longer than an hour? Oh, that's right I *did* forget to mention that part, did I not? My bad, MUAHAHAHA!!!" It was the nefarious Secondras and he was teasing the king in his own wicked ways again. "By the way, those two royal guards were delicious, thanks for the treat! You really shouldn't have you know, muahaha! Could have used a little salt and vinegar there, but whatever!" There was something about their flesh being tough and almost hard to swallow as the evil voice trailed off. Those two royal guards (once, sadly) guarding the king's private chamber were some of the strongest and toughest guards in the entire magical fantasy kingdom, complete with huge muscular bodies. So, of course they were tough! And who in their right minds would eat them!!!

Admitting defeat, King Devonus slumped down on his king-sized waterbed, or what remained of it, both hands covering his jaded face. He had lost, the young king thought to himself. Why did he even bother in the first place? His arch nemesis was no ordinary man. The king wasn't even sure if he was going against a man anymore. Secondras the Warlock had proven himself time and time again to be far too powerful for any man to deal with, even for mighty kings like him. King Devonus was just about at his wit's end when he heard the resonant cries of a baby not far away. Normally the king would have cringed with fright and disgust at the cries of his yet-to-be-named baby boy. But this time, he sat up straight and his face lit up as a plan started to take shape in his chaotic mind.

When he was but still a boy, King Devonus would often sneak out of the royal palace late at night disguised as a lowly servant boy accompanied by his most trusted personal bodyguard, also in disguise as his pet. It was a noble yet nasty canine of a Doberman whose bite, contrary to popular belief as those who were unfortunate enough to find out the painful and bloody way, was a lot worse than its bark.

The young prince Devonus loved to explore the many ancient ruins and natural forests in his kingdom. It was during one of his nightly escapades that he discovered an ancient ruin with a funny-looking door standing all alone in the middle of a broken room. There were weird runes on both sides of the door and a hexagram symbol on the ground of the front and back of the door as well. Nothing unusual happened when the boy prince opened the door on both sides. So he copied the runes that were on either sides of the door which he firmly believed were magical incantations to activate whatever purpose or purposes the door was meant for.

It wasn't until two years later, after much research going through the old and dusty books on sorcery and magical runes, incantations and the likes in the royal library, that the teenaged prince finally discovered the secrets behind the lonesome weird door that did not seem to lead anywhere.

He was fourteen then and already exhibiting signs of the fine young man he would soon become. After much experimentation by citing different versions of the same runes later, the teenaged prince

Devonus had come to the conclusion that the door was indeed no ordinary door. Instead, what he had found presumably by fate, was a magical portal that lead to numerous fascinating lands with funny exotic names like America, Japan, China, India, Russia, Australia, Germany, Thailand, New Zealand, Malaysia and a tiny island not many people had heard of - yet; Singapore. And that was the country King Devonus had made up his mind to send his newborn son to before the vile Secondras could lay his claw-like hands on him. He had the strangest notion that his son would be safe there until he was of a suitable age to return home and hopefully assist the king in defeating the atrocious and obviously very much insane Secondras the Warlock.

A few days had passed since the mad warlock's visit to King Devonus. During that short duration the young king spent as much time as he could bonding with his new baby son and even came up with a name for him. The day to fulfill his promise to Secondras had arrived. But the king had no wish to honor his promise. Honoring it would only mean certain doom for his only son and heir to his kingdom. So why would he do that!

It was slightly past midnight as the young king stood in the ruins where the portal was located, with the baby Crown Prince wrapped in a soft piece of yellow cloth safe in his arms. Placed inside the bundle with the Crown Prince was a small piece of paper that read (in, yes, English), "His name is Dave. Please take good care of him, for he is unlike most others."

The night air that was still before begun to stir, lightly at first and then picking up speed as King Devonus recited a powerful spell that would open the portal to a different world where Prince Dave, his son, would lead a commoner's life for many years before he would return to the kingdom of *Phantasy* as the Crown Prince and rightful heir to the throne. At least he would be safe from the dark tentacles of Secondras's influence and demonic minions that could never reach him there, or so the young king thought.

No sooner had baby Dave been safely delivered to his destination in another world, a loud thunder was heard and a single huge lighting struck the perimeter of the ruins where King Devonus was.

"Aww shit! What have you done, my dear King Devonus! Ah, but then again, that's expected. Congratulations, your Majesty, you have just fulfilled the third part of the prophecy, muahahaha!!!" With that said and done, Secondras the Warlock faded away as suddenly as he had appeared.

"What do you mean?" cried a confused King Devonus. All that answered him now was the deathly silence of the night, and the occasional creepy noises made by the unknown creatures that roamed that part of the kingdom during that period, creeping here and there, minding their own businesses and watching the king's every move.

That was the last that King Devonus saw and heard from his arch nemesis. It wasn't until many, many years later that they met again and during that peaceful period, the kingdom of *Phantasy* flourished under the rule of King Devonus who aged wisely and graciously. He never remarried even though many fine and lovely princesses and even a queen or two and countless beautiful, rich and influential ladies of noble birth from far and wide sought his attention. King Devonus was a devoted and hopelessly passionate man indeed with only Queen Katrina being his one true love.

(This concludes Chapter 1.)

CHAPTER 2:

MEET DAVE, THE COMMONER PRINCE.

In the blink of an eye (and the flip of a page), fifteen years have passed since the epic events in the kingdom of *Phantasy* (pronounced *Fee-yond-derr-see*), a magical faraway fairy-tale land, involving a king (Devonus), a demented warlock (Secondras) and a baby prince (Dave). And of course, not forgetting a tiny island not many people had heard of then; the Republic of Singapore. Or simply Singapore, as it is known today.

Indeed, fifteen years have passed since the baby crown prince Dave was transported via occult means to Singapore and it was there that he spent his childhood and teenage years. Little of him was known back in his own world. And even less was known of him in the foreign land that he was raised by his foster parents.

King Devonus had done his part as a father by placing his newborn baby prince at the front door of a poor and childless yet nonetheless contented couple. To most people, that might have seemed like a heartless act for a father to do. But it was indeed the right thing to do then, placing the life of his only son in the capable hands of strangers in another world. Many would have argued that who knew how they would treat him, for Prince Dave was not the flesh and blood of the commoner couple King Devonus entrusted his son to. After all, had there not been countless horror stories of the most evil treatment awarded to children not theirs? Cinderella is one such famous example. Ah, but fear not, for King Devonus was one far-sighted and smart man who planned well ahead.

Unbeknownst to those back in the Land of the Beyond, the young king had been taking frequent trips in secret to the many other wondrous and incredible lands that were revealed to him one by one during the span of his long life ever since his fateful discovery of the magical door portal that seemed to lead to nowhere. He had always avoided unwanted attention whenever he journeyed to the many foreign and unknown lands by wearing the clothes he found scattered throughout them, usually through discreet means, if you know what I mean. Devonus might be a king in his own rights, but he was trained as a soldier too. And being a soldier as well as a king, Devonus was just doing what's natural and necessary for survival in unknown hostile environments.

During his numerous journeys to all those interesting places, King Devonus appeared humble and every inch a civilian, divulging nothing of the royal blood that ran beneath his skin. Who would have believed that he was actually a real king from a magical faraway fantasy kingdom visiting their countries via a magical portal and without a passport? He would have easily been deemed an illegal immigrant with a vivid imagination, thrown into jail and deported back to where he came from, wherever that was! He made many new friends that way and learned much about the distinct and diverse cultures, backgrounds and languages that they had to offer. And being the wise king that he was, King Devonus was indeed a fast learner! But that's another story altogether, of course.

So what has King Devonus's magical travels to the different lands we know so well got to do with his son Prince Dave and his future? As mentioned earlier, King Devonus ventured far and wide into hostile territories that he had absolutely no knowledge of. But there was this land, actually a really, really tiny island nothing more than a red speck on the world map, controlled not by a king but rather, most peculiarly by a body of intelligent people voted unanimously by their supporters, that caught his attention and quite impressed him. This 'body of people', made up of a mixture of the different races of people living in Singapore, was known as a 'government', which was, of course, unheard of in the kingdom of *Phantasy*.

Singapore, although a young and tiny nation, was a safe and secure haven gratified by its low crime rate, which was exactly what was required to keep King Devonus's son safe and sound for as long and as far away from the likes of his arch nemesis Secondras as possible. Besides, the citizens of Singapore, known as Singaporeans, were generally a friendly, generous, encouraging and somewhat funny cosmopolitan lot. In fact, they were so proud of their mixed and diverse cultures and heritages, they had created an entire language of their own called 'Singlish', somewhat slightly similar to the universal language English, which was never officially recognized as a language in its own right, and not really approved and encouraged either by its firm and stringent government. It was a most peculiar language punctuated sparingly by weird nouns and adjectives such as 'leh', 'lah', 'ley', 'lor', 'wor', 'meh' and 'hor', which never failed to leave King Devonus behaving in a rather unkingly manner by laughing out loudly (lol). But then again, he was never a king during such travels, just your regular average joe kind of guy.

It was during one such frequent visit to Singapore that the young king had the luck to chance upon and become very good friends with the childless couple who would one day become the adopted parents of Prince Dave. It was a fated affair and King Devonus had no idea then of the significant part they would play later.

That happened some time before he met, fell madly in love with and married Katrina, had Dave, and became a young widower. All within the span of two short years, after he met his one true love Katrina, that is.

Now, this barren couple had tried for many years different and various means of having a child of their own, from the tried and tested conventional methods to the creepier and darker ones. They had visited all the doctors they knew, taken all sorts of western medicines with funny names they had never even heard of and Chinese prescriptions of unfamiliar and weird-looking herbs and even tiger penises and bull testicles recommended by their relatives and friends. There was even once they visited this powerful Malay bomoh (a witch doctor who, in most cases, grants the sinister wishes of his clients through the unorthodox means of black magic. There are good ones who heal too, though rarer than their darker counterparts.) who resided somewhere in the remote wilderness of Indonesia. Still nothing! Well, there was that one time the wife was pregnant but as fate would have it, she suffered a miscarriage under mysterious circumstances and was sadly unable to conceive again.

They finally gave up all hopes of having children of their own and were too poor to adopt one the legal way. And since they didn't wish to spend the rest of what remained of their misery lives behind bars, they remained childless and were not really enthusiastic about it at all. But they were a couple of nice people and managed as best as they could, no doubt the long and hard way. One of their favorite pastimes was to feed the forever hungry stray cats that made their homes at the void deck below their HDB flat. They treated these felines as if they were their own children and even gave names to the more active and sociable ones which never failed to respond when they were called. So you can imagine how their peaceful world was turned upside down the night they found this adorable newborn baby boy at the front of their door wrapped in an oddly soft yellow cloth with a note in standard English that read "His name is Dave. Please take good care of him, for he is unlike most others." That was how this ordinary childless couple's life changed forever with the arrival of the baby Prince Dave.

Of course, they didn't know then the 'abandoned' baby was a real prince from another world. Maybe they wouldn't have accepted him if they knew. But to this couple, a baby's a baby, prince or alien or whatever he was. And that was how Prince Dave came to live the life of a commoner suffering in poverty in a land far, far away so unlike the one from the very first day he was born where his ancestors lived a life purely of luxury and glory from the day they were born to the day they died, which common poor folks can only experience in their dreams (like me, the author, for instance)!

But the story does not end here of course, for there's more in store. As a matter of fact, the real tale of how Dave the last prince of *Phantasy* saved his kingdom from the evil clutches of the heinous and totally twisted warlock who called himself Secondras is just about to commence!

(This concludes Chapter 2.)

CHAPTER 3:

ENTER AND DISAPPEAR UNCLE JONES.

Not so very often something out of the blue comes along and disrupts our life in a way that we least expect. It may or may not be a good thing, we never know for sure, until it has happened. It might appear in the form of a miracle (please take note a miracle may not always be a good thing for it may still end horribly wrong with disastrous results!) or disaster or a blessing in disguise even (a blessing in disguise, however, is a good thing for it always ends with a positive ending, hence the given expression).

But that was exactly how the Teos felt when they opened their standard-issued and very plain wooden front door of their rented two-room HDB flat located somewhere in the neighborhood of Chai Chee one fine dawn...and discovered to their utmost shock and surprise, a mysterious little bundle (of joy) wrapped in the softest and smoothest piece of silky cloth they had ever felt that was the color of the fiery sun.

Even more puzzling was the tiny piece of white paper with its neat handwriting that said in, yes, perfect English: "His name is Dave. Please take good care of him, for he is unlike most others."

Stunned as the poor but contented and industrious couple were at what was the biggest discovery of their lives so far, they regained their senses soon enough and concurred that the handwriting on the note that came with the baby was somehow oddly familiar. It was obvious that the baby belonged to the owner of that handwritten strange piece of note. Besides, the fragrance on it smelled like an old acquaintance of theirs they had not seen or heard from in a very, very long time indeed. The Teos should know for he was the only one they ever knew who wore such an alluringly one-of-a-kind exotic perfume that reminded them of his amazing-yet-true tales of far-away lands from beyond the reaches of ordinary poor folks like themselves.

The Teos was an educated but poor and humbled couple who had met in their mid teens. Rebellious, ambitious, confused, curious and somewhat lost like most teenagers, they decided the only way out was to elope when their parents found out about their illicit relationship and forbade them from seeing each other (they truly loved each other and were too smart to commit suicide).

Michael Teo Boon Heng was originally from a wealthy family who's sole breadwinner was Teo Soon Huat, a true-blue shrewd and ruthless businessman who accumulated his wealth from the sales of coffee beans from his numerous coffee plantations scattered all over Malaysia, Indonesia and Thailand, some of which he had acquired through unorthodox means from his rivals. He was also one of the richest man in the Singapore of his era and unfortunately enough, the heartless father of Michael Teo.

Michael's dad disowned him the day he ran away from home and started a new life with his then girlfriend, Michelle Ng Siew Lan. After all, the elder Teo reasoned that he had three legally-married wives, five openly acknowledged mistresses, twenty-one legitimate sons and four daughters and god knows how many more illegitimate children out there he has had with his countless flings and flashy one-night stands. So what was the loss of one useless son who chose to disobey and disgrace him by marrying the smelly daughter of a poor farmer who was of a class way, way beneath his? But he was gracious enough to let Michael keep his family name even though Michael's tyrant of a dad thought he had dishonored it by falling in love with a dirty, stinking and poor farmer's daughter, and even going as far as to elope with her!

The elder Teo had even harbored secret thoughts that one of the sons he favored the most, Michael, would tire of that poor farmer girl soon enough and come begging on all fours to be let back into the comfy posh lifestyle that he had so grown accustomed to since his birth. But that event became old Teo Soon Huat's sole wishful thinking and he died without one last look at the apple of his eye; a sad and lonely old man who laid bedridden on his deathbed, full of regrets, surrounded by idiots and hypocrites who only pleased him just to win his favor as they hungered after and fought over the immense wealth that old Teo would leave behind after his demise. (Do keep in mind that this happened in an era long past, back in the 'good old' 1960s of the then newly independent Singapore about twenty years after World War II where discrimination against the poor by the filthy rich was nothing short of an everyday affair.)

Michelle Teo Siew Lan, who's maiden name was simply Ng Siew Lan, or Siow Lan as she was fondly addressed by her closest family members, on the other hand, was the second eldest child of a family of eight. Born to a farmer father and housewife mother with six young mouths to feed constantly, it was a relieve rather to both her parents when she broke the sad news to them as that meant one less mouth to feed. Her eighteen year-old elder brother, Ng Ah Kow, had already left the slow and peaceful kampong lifestyle where everyone knew each other and were truly friendly and helpful. He was sad but proud at the same time to have been the first batch of Singaporeans enlisted in the newly established SAF two years back and army life in those days was very tough and a lot stringent and so much different compared to the technologically advanced comfy army lifestyle we see today. (Remember what 'field days' in those days were like for the old-timers?)

It was by fate that they had met, both Michael and Michelle, and it was Michael who gave Michelle Teo her English name. Michelle

Teo had been a comely lass when she first met her then boyfriend and present husband and the name "Michelle" simply came into Michael's mind when he first set eyes on her. It wasn't really love at first sight for the two lovebirds and they had their differences initially since they both came from very different backgrounds. But they learned to accommodate each other with every passing day and thus, their passion for each other stood the test of time. And so it was also fate that had brought the tiny bundle of joy that was Dave, the Commoner Prince, into the lonely but otherwise, contented lives of the infertile couple. Finally, their prayers had been answered, though somewhat in a rather unexpected and surprising manner. But a gift of God was a gift of God nonetheless.

The Teo's lives turned upside down immediately after the tiny toddler came without warning into their lives. Michael was a bus-driver who worked extra hard, even covering for his colleagues when necessary and Michelle, an office cleaner-lady who was fortunate enough to find work in one of the offices nearby their rented flat. They worked really hard to bring their only son up and putting him through school. The first few years were the most trying, especially when they had almost no experience in taking care of a child, except for Michelle who had taken care of her younger siblings before while her father toiled long and hard under the hot blazing sun in the fields from dawn to dusk and her mother worked equally hard taking care of the house and what few farm animals they had and putting their three daily meals together.

When Dave had just turned ten, the Teos moved out of their rented two-room flat and into a rented three-room flat in the same neighborhood. Well, actually all they did was simply shift to a slightly bigger flat a few units away from their old one on the same level in the same block of flats which was no big deal really. Dave was growing up after all and reaching puberty soon at that time and his parents thought it was only natural he had his own bedroom even though it was but just a small tiny room with a small excuse of a hole for a window. But to Dave it opened up a whole new world of possibilities for him as that meant he now had his very own privacy where he could do as he wished sans the ever watchful eyes of his parents, especially his over-protective mom. But then again that wasn't always the case as he was ordered to open his door at all times while Dave was in his room by both parents.

And so, in the twinkle of an eye, fifteen years zoomed by just like that and little Dave was little no more. He was now a bespectacled and pudgy young lad of fifteen who resembled nothing like either of his parents, or somebody that his parents knew really. Even their long-time neighbors still had no idea where he had suddenly appeared from and why. All they knew was that the childless Teos next door had suddenly become the proud parents of a healthy baby boy overnight and for them, it was even better than striking 4D or TOTO or any other form of lottery for that matter.

The teenager known as Dave Teo Chen Lee with a mystery past he had no idea of, went to school just like any ordinary kids. He looked every inch normal enough. He spoke and acted without any sign of oddities and his (foster) parents were relieved for that. But little did they realize that things were about to change shortly after Dave had reached his fifteenth birthday and the boy they had brought up as their own wasn't just another typical average human boy. No, in fact, his (royal and troublesome) past was about to catch up to him and poor clueless Dave was about to go for the ride of his young life!

Even though Dave had already reached the 'ripe old' age of fifteen, his social life was just another myth and all the friends he had were of the imaginary type where only he himself could see and hear them. They were all in his mind of course but did he care? Even in school, he isolated himself from the rest of his schoolmates (not just classmates, mind you) and teachers and opened his big fat mouth only when he had to answer questions from his teachers, or during recess time when he would buy his favorite Hainanese chicken rice (one of Singapore's favorite and famous dishes which he seemingly never got sick of) and sit in a remote corner of his school canteen and eat alone, oblivious to the rest of the activities around him as usual.

Because of his indifferent and aloof nature, which was always misunderstood as arrogance, Dave was often the target of his school bullies. Nobody ever stopped to help him in the face of danger, not even the teachers as nobody pitied him. All his schoolmates and teachers and even the school principal were under the misconception that he was just another rotten spoilt brat from a rich family who looked down on everybody else. They were wrong of course. In reality, Dave was no more a conceited and spoiled misunderstood teenager then the poor homeless beggars on the streets. He was the shy, quiet type of person who didn't know how to express himself, especially in the company of his peers, and girls, really! In short, Dave was no more than just a fifteen year-old loser of the typical teenage boy with average looks and no skills, no dreams and no hope that everybody can identify with but never really want to point their finger at. And things would have remained that way had the school janitor not decided to interfere eventually.

He was a portly man with a balding head usually hidden under an oversized straw hat and a snow-white foot-long beard. Standing tall at 1.95m with broad shoulders and tanned muscular arms and legs, Uncle Jones was an Eurasian of sorts who didn't look anything like the average school janitor found in most schools at all. Instead and indeed, he reminded most people of the wrestlers from the good old (and now defunct) WWF (remember this was all back in the good old 80s). Though already sixty-seven, he was still popular among the female school teachers and even more so among the female students studying at Upper Cross Secondary School.

Uncle Jones was the only person Dave actually talked to in school and they made an odd couple whenever they were seen together, not unlike the Dynamic Duo Batman and Robin, minus the costumes and fancy gears and gadgets of course. Dave confided in Uncle Jones all his troubles in school as well as his dreams and fantasies. Uncle Jones would help Dave in his studies and homework whenever he could. They usually hung out together during recess time in the mini school garden which was one of Uncle Jones's proudest achievements as the school janitor of Upper Cross Secondary School. Although tropically small, the school garden was full of colorful flowers and potted plants and even some chairs to sit in and admire its simple yet beautiful surroundings, courtesy of Uncle Jones. It was a well potted and maintained little garden and weeds were uprooted when spotted.

Dave felt a strange affinity toward the school janitor which he had no explanation for no matter how hard he tried. Uncle Jones was a father-figure to Dave and queerly enough, he thought of Uncle Jones more as a father than his own (foster father whom he had no idea was not his real father at that time) and instead of pushing that weird thought away, Dave unabashedly welcomed it with a broad silly lopsided grin every time that thought crossed his mind. Maybe it was all just a coincidence but whatever it was, both Uncle Jones and Dave did share some uncanny habits and resemblances. They both had the same thick bushy eyebrows (though of different colors; the older man had greyish-white eyebrows while the young one's were black), big shiny brown eyes and they both shared that same faraway, dreamy look when they were deep in their own thoughts. But that was where the similarities ended: one was a short and plumb boy who wore a pair of cheap plastic glasses flamed by thick, black rims while the other was a balding yet smartly-dressed old man in a class of his own who had to constantly bend his head when talking to the teenager.

It could only be assumed that there was hope for Dave yet with the appearance of Uncle Jones to guide him in his young and disturbed teenage life. But alas, nothing was ever permanent and all things must come to an end, even the good times. Dave had barely started his third year into his secondary school and he was so looking forward to spending more quality time with his godfather; Uncles Jones, when the bad news came in a rather unexpected manner. Uncle Jones had quit as the janitor of Upper Cross Secondary School, just like that! The official reason given was that he had to settle some problems back home which needed his much attention. Which was a mystery to everyone at Upper Cross Secondary School and poor Dave was no exception. Never had Uncle Jones mentioned anything about his family or where he came from. Not even once and not even to Dave whom he had come to regard as his own son (the truth was even closer than anyone could imagine actually).

The news of Uncle Jones's sudden disappearance came barely one month after Dave had past his fifteenth birthday. Dave reverted to his old former lonesome self. There were no more smiles and laughter from him. The twinkle in his eyes faded away into the nothingness they had come from. He now spent all of his recess time hidden in a quiet corner of the school library, burying his face in the fantasy and science-fiction books that Uncle Jones had introduced to him, far and away from the boisterous lively crowds of school children outside, lost in an entire world of his own. He slouched more than before, especially when walking, or rather, dragging his feet along. Not even the constant nagging of Dave's mother was able to change anything. The sight of the mini school garden only reminded Dave of the happier times he had spent with Uncle Jones and he avoided it altogether when he could. Thus the school garden grew unkempt as time went by for the new school janitor was a lazy young man who knew nothing about gardening.

"Come on, principal Goh, you *must* know where Uncle Jones has gone to! I beg of you! Think hard, he must have mentioned where he was going, right?" Dave was pleading desperately to his school principal, Mr. Vincent Goh in his luxurious air-conditioned office the same day the news was released.

"Well, I'm really sorry, Dave. I know how close you and old man Jones were but believe me when I tell you he never said anything about where he came from or where he was headed. In fact, he hardly mentioned a word about his family or private life to me, not that I never inquired from him."

Vincent Goh pondered hard for a while and then his face lit up with a puzzled look.

"Wait a minute...I remember something now. I believe he did mention something about an emergency of a grave magnitude demanding his immediate attention had suddenly popped up out of nowhere and he had to return urgently to settle it. Oh... He was going back to what he called...the...Land of the Beyond, wherever that is!" the school principal shrugged nonchalantly at Dave while taking his own sweet time to divulge the important details he had kept from him. (What a dirty little weasel Dave's school principal was!)

"What...? A place called 'The Land of the Beyond'? That's it? He never mentioned anything else?!! Not even anything remotely related to me? Such as 'Goodbye, Dave' or 'See you later, Dave'?"

Dave was clearly flustered as his face flushed bright red. He was curious as he wondered what disaster could have befallen unto his Uncle Jones that required his immediate attention without bidding even a simple farewell to his favorite godson before leaving (for good?).

"What?!! Why are you still here in my office! Get out! Now!!!" the balding middle-aged Vincent Goh screamed as Dave hurriedly left the principal's office.

(This concludes Chapter 3.)

CHAPTER 4:

THEY AWAIT.

"**G**o away, please!"
      "Leave me alone!"

"Why are you following me? What did I ever do to you?!!"

The pleading voice was small and weak and belonged to a short flabby figure trying his utmost best to run away from something or things, rather, terrifying. Close on his heels were three huge pairs of red eyes that glowed menacingly in the dark. The running figure tripped and fell flat on his face. The three gigantic silhouettes that were straddling along behind caught up to the fallen shape in no time at all and as one colossal hairy claw of a hand reached out to grab the fallen form...

That was when Dave managed to wake up with a start. Numerous beads of perspiration were flowing down his forehead and his body kept quivering uncontrollably as if he was trapped in a freezer. The recurring nightmare had begun almost immediately for Dave after Uncle Jones disappeared inscrutably and abruptly and without so much as a "Good-bye" or "See ya!" even.

The nightmare was always the same. It always started every single night after Dave had trouble falling into deep slumber with the teenager running away from three hulking humanoid shapes with glowing red-hot eyes the size of tennis balls and ending up

with him tripping over something he can never see in the dark –
and a humongous clumsy hand hairy-as-can-be (which never failed
to remind Dave of a tree branch full of sharp and pointed leaves)
reaching out to grab him... And every single night it appeared to be
closing in by an inch or so. That's when Dave never failed to wake
up at that crucial point of his nightmare. Like, what gives, man?

Dave shuddered to think what would have happened had
they really caught hold of him. Would he really be trapped in that
nightmare and never wake up again???!!! Of course that would never
become true, right? It's all just a nightmare and that's all there was
to it, Dave laughed it off shakily, or was it...? It seemed so real
though, Dave could even smell the rotten breaths of those three dark
creatures as they closed in on him. By the way, their breaths truly
stank! The offensive odor lingered long after Dave had woken up
from his nightmare. Was it *just* a nightmare? Hmmm...

4.45am, showed the hands of the analogue alarm clock beside
Dave's single-bed mattress on the floor as he glanced at it. Dave's
(foster) parents were too poor to afford a proper bed for him so
he had to content with a thick mattress instead but Dave was an
understanding boy who didn't mind as long as he had a roof over
his head, and his books. To the young teenage boy, his fantasy and
science-fiction books were all that mattered to him at that point in
his young, troubled life.

There were a couple of hours left till the break of dawn (roughly
around 06:40am) and Dave was feeling rather restless. He couldn't
fall back to sleep again and the night was warm despite the twelve-
inch fan blowing furiously at its highest speed in his face, next to
his hot, sweaty body. The June month-long school holiday was
here again and Dave could not hide his excitement as he laid on
his mattress thinking about his favorite pastime (reading) and his
favorite hangout of all times – the newly renovated and fully air-
conditioned neighborhood library with its freshly acquired twelve
thousand recycled books for all ages and genres.

The time was now nine in the morning and Dave was looking fresh as a daisy and full of energy as he prepared to step out of the house. He was dressed in his favorite khaki Bermuda shorts and white tee-shirt with the huge silly orange grinning face of Dave's favorite cat, Garfield, printed on its front. Dave had already taken his breakfast of toast with butter and kaya (a favorite and common breakfast among Singaporeans, especially the older generation) and washed it down with his usual cup of English tea. He had his small bottle of water with him as he set out for his favorite haunt. It was a good thing the newly renovated local library came equipped with new water coolers situated outside all of its toilets on every floor which meant free water refills. Unfortunately though, drinking and eating were forbidden in the library itself. Nonetheless, someone was smart enough to incorporate a cafeteria into the newly refurbished library where you can sit all day in comfort and eat and drink as much as you wanted, till the café or the library closed for the day, whichever came first, of course.

"Don't be late for dinner again, son," Dave's mother called out after him as he stepped out of their rented three-room flat somewhere in the district of Chai Chee.

"You are always making me worry so much for you, Dave," Michelle Teo continued as her voice landed on deaf ears. "You know you always do, son." Michelle was genuinely worried for the safety of her only son as all mothers were, even though Dave was not her own flesh and blood.

Michelle Teo was forced to quit her cleaner job and focus as a full-time housewife and mother less than a year after Dave had silently but surely intruded into their lives. She found out the hard way it was never a good idea to let their inquisitive immediate neighbor babysit the new treasure in their lives as she simply asked too many questions and there was no shutting her up, besides killing her. Since killing was illegal and took too much trouble and time cleaning up after, the Teos decided to give up on that idea, not that they didn't give it much thought though. Their neighbor, a certain madam Fauzia Bte Ahmad, also a housewife like Michelle, was certainly a pain in the neck (and butt) most of the times as she was such a busybody always gossiping and minding other peoples' businesses! In the end, it was up to Michael Teo, who earned his living as a public bus-driver, to support his family of three. He had done a wonderful job as a husband and father so far and there was no looking back.

"Ya, I won't lah, ma," was Dave's usual curt reply.

Within two or three minutes, depending on how busy the lifts were, he was away from the block of flats that had been home to Dave for the last fifteen years of his life, and probably more to come. The distance from Dave's house to his newly refurbished neighborhood library wasn't that far away. It was still within walking distance even though it took Dave an average of fifteen to twenty minutes to reach it via walking. And it was a habit of Dave to hum quietly to himself while being oblivious to everything else as he walked along.

There was this particular small hill which Dave had to cross in order to get to his favorite chill-out place and although it wasn't that big an area as it was more of a park really, it seemed to take forever for Dave that exceptional morning to get across it. It was already halfway past eleven am and the day was starting to turn hotter just as Dave was about to give up and head in the direction he thought was home. Well, there were still some of his favorite fantasy and science-fiction books he had bought dirt-cheap the other day from the book fair in school before it closed for the month-long school holiday and he could dig into those, if he couldn't find anything else better to do.

It was at that point in time when Dave was still contemplating in his mind what to do when he heard...the Voices! It was a fact Dave grew up on fairy tales and mystical beings such as dragons, fairies, trolls, orcs, ogres, giants, unicorns and pixies. But to actually be able to eavesdrop on a surreal conversation about them while being lost in an area he had grown so accustomed to since he had learned to walk was a bit too much for Dave even!

Dave's initial reaction after he had gotten over the shock was that it was all a dream and he must have felt drowsy and fallen asleep while crossing the hill to the other side to where his objective, the local neighborhood library was. After all, Dave reasoned that it had happened to him before so it might as well have occurred again! So he slapped and bit himself – and felt very silly after that. It was still daylight and the beautiful day was just beginning as proven by his Casio watch which was showing that it was now forty-five minutes passed eleven in the morning. And the weirdest part of all was that Dave could still hear the unearthly voices!

The voices sounded distant yet clear, like it was coming from the other side of the hill, where the library, his favorite destination was. Curiosity soon got the better of him and Dave began to head toward the direction in which he thought the alien voices were coming from. As Dave strained his ears and listened intently, the voices became clearer and Dave came to the conclusion they belonged to two adults, both male with a very weird accent he had never heard of before. The two voices did not seem local and sounded somewhat from a place far, far away.

From what little bits and pieces of the supernatural conversation Dave could hear, he deduced that they were talking about mythical creatures and such. But why would they? These mythical beings Dave knew so well only existed in the fairy-tales and nowhere else! Dave paused and hesitated, not sure if he should continue walking in his intended direction. The idea of the safety of his little bedroom where he could be lost in his own fantasy world of dragons, knights in shinning armor on flying horses and damsels in distress appeared very tempting indeed. Then a myriad of "What if" questions starting pouring through Dave's mind. The fear of real imminent danger weighed heavily in our young hero's heart. Yet before he even realized it, as if they had a mind of their own, Dave's feet were already halfway through the hill and the deep longing for a real adventure soon got the better of him!

However, before Dave could take another step, a white cloud of smoke appeared from out of nowhere and poor Dave was lost within it!

After it had suddenly vanished just as mysteriously as it had appeared, Dave found himself in the presence of two very funny-looking and unusual characters indeed! For standing before him now were this really huge and tall talking dog (a Doberman to be exact) and what appeared to be a giant broken egg pieced together in a rather unprofessional way! Gone was the familiar background Dave had grown so accustomed to. Instead and indeed, he now found himself standing in the middle of a big open plain grass field, along with his two new companions.

The weird-looking Egg-man was the first to open his mouth with his freakishly high-pitched voice. "Well, there you are, your Highness! I hope the short trip back home did nothing to faze your nerves, aye!" Egg-man made an obvious wink at the poor stunned Dave, then turned to his vertically-unchallenged dog-like mate and said under his breath, "Are you positive that's him, Musscus?"

To which Musscus, the dog-like man creature, simply and calmly replied in his deep guff voice, "Should be, no doubt about that, Hootus my man. Smells like our 'long-lost' prince too."

Dave blinked his eyes several times but the ridiculous scene that was slowly unfolding before his very eyes not unlike a page out of a fantasy book (ironically that *is* what is happening now as you read this) continued and refused to go away. Gradually but surely, the helpless teenager came to the strange (but true?) conclusion that he had been abducted by aliens dressed in silly costumes and there was no way home for him. Worse still, what experiments were they going to perform on him he wondered?

"Oh wait, this can't be true... I have to be day-dreaming again! I must be... This is all so surreal it can't be happening to me. Not now, I'm still so young and there's so much more I have yet to do, and, and places to go, people to see..." thought Dave as panic and confusion started to take hold of his consciousness.

"NO!!!" screamed a helpless Dave who dropped on all fours. What was going on, really! He could breathe and smell the fresh grass beneath his open palms. His heart was pumping faster and faster than before and he could feel that...

The two strangers who looked like they had stepped out of a page from the fantasy books he had grown so used to were still standing before him as he looked up at them with big, bewildered eyes. They had even greeted him the first time he'd set eyes on them, which was like, two minutes ago only.

After what seemed like an eternity which, in reality, was no more than five minutes, Dave finally found his voice and asked timidly.

"So, are you guys for real?"

(This concludes Chapter 4.)

Chapter 5:

THE ICE-BREAKING.

All sorts of funny and weird thoughts were running amok through Dave's still confused mind as he tried to evaluate the situation he wished he was not in. His head was spinning hard like a rotating top that didn't want to stop. Everything around him now felt totally surreal.

Dave could see the Egg-man shooting his mouth non-stop in front of him but he couldn't even focus on a single word Hootus was saying. His vision was starting to blur again, which lasted only a mere few seconds yet felt like an eternity (not again!). And when the poor lost teenager regained his vision, the two misfits from out of nowhere were still standing tall and proud within reach.

Egg-man Hootus was wearing what could only be perceived as a cross between a concerned and a confounded look on his face with a raised eyebrow above extraordinarily large round eyes whereas his dog-like companion's facial expression remained absolutely rigid and unchanged.

If Musscus was a dog, he sure didn't act like one. Dogs, no matter the species and size, were supposed to be gregarious and friendly animals (now remember this, I said 'supposed to be', not that all dogs really have to be sociable creatures, just generally speaking, that's all), especially the tamed ones who were used to the company of humans.

Yet here was a dog that appeared to be a Doberman standing on his two hind legs, slightly taller than the average basketball player, who might not have appeared as fierce as dogs his size would. But then again, Musscus wasn't exactly what anyone could term as "your typical four-legged man's best friend" type of dog. Dave had not the faintest of clue then, but ole Musscus (who was really only a few years older than Dave himself in the human years) would be the one to constantly save his princely butt soon, and not just smelling it.

There was something rather oddly familiar about the Doberman Dog-man called Musscus. It was like Dave had seen him somewhere before and yet he just couldn't quite figure out where. Without his realizing it, Dave was staring most intently at the composed and lanky still figure in front of him, trying his best to read the Dog-man's thoughts through his big soft brown eyes. Dave realized that he had seen such a stony look very much like the one on Musscus before.

Although not really a fan of one of the world's greatest invention since its debut with almost every household in the world having at least one; the television, Dave did watch once in a while even though there was none at his home since his parents were that poor. He had witnessed movies (in shopping malls and coffee-shops) where big-sized bodyguards wearing cool-looking sunglasses with bulging muscles stood statue-still while watching over their charges like birds-of-prey, never taking their eyes off them even for a mere second.

And that was the same exact feeling Musscus gave Dave as they both stood staring at each other, as if sizing the other up, like two hot-blooded cowboys just before a showdown. But what was a poor flustered teenager like Dave, lost in a foreign land like none he had actually ever seen or been to before, know anyway? And wait...did that Egg-man Hootus just address him as 'Prince Dave'? Wow...but no, wait! This was all getting too good to be true and too much for Dave to handle all at once and his head was starting to spin again...

His very own fantasy-adventure came true? Can it truly be?

The next thing Dave knew, he was in Musscus's strong, steely arms and that felt so good, yet so wrong!

"No, no! This is not right!" exclaimed an exasperated Dave as he pulled himself hurriedly away from Musscus.

"I mean, why am I here? Who are you jokers and why did you kidnap me, man!" our young and confused hero demanded.

Then he leaned close to Hootus, looked straight into the Eggman and tried to simulate the way he raised one of his eyebrows. "You two weirdoes...aren't from Singapore, are you?"

"...Sing...Singa...pore?" Hootus wore a stunned look on his face as he continued (it was obvious at this point who among the two was the better talker, and liar). "No, no, your Highness, we aren't, wherever that may be (Hootus shot a knowing wink at his Dogman companion). Look, we were just following orders and our top priority was to bring *you*", Hootus nodded his head respectfully in Dave's direction as he said this, "the rightful heir to the throne of this dying kingdom, *Phantasy*, home safely after your fifteenth birthday and that's all we know, seriously!" Hootus raised both hands high in the air dramatically as he said this.

"Hmm, is that so? I know I may look stupid and even act dumb at times but I'm NOT, okay! You guys had better tell me the truth like who you really are, where you come from, and where this place is right now or...or I'll call the police, you got that?!!"

It was Hootus's and Musscus's turn now to look confused (well, more amused than anything else actually) and they weren't hiding that from Dave. It was written clearly all over their stunned faces.

"The, the police? What's that? Some kind of 'Singapore' joke, your Highness?" asked a very puzzled Hootus as he edged the side of Musscus with his elbow while wearing a sort of smirk on his broken face. It was clear Hootus was playing along with Dave and he was enjoying every bit of it!

As the fog in his mind cleared, it became certain to Dave that he had been brought to a foreign land against his will without his consent and he was probably knocked unconscious before the journey began and had come to his senses only when his abductors were discussing fervently about his future (which was true actually) in a rather loud and obnoxious manner in an open grass field in the middle of nowhere. Maybe they were trying to wake him up in a rather indirect manner. But then again, what's up with the silly costumes? It wasn't like it was Halloween or anything...or was it?

At this point Dave glanced casually at his watch and to his mortification his one and only prized black digital Casio watch had stopped functioning! It was the only watch Dave had ever possessed and it was a birthday present he had received from his parents on his twelfth birthday and for passing his PSLE as well. It was also one of the most expensive items Dave had ever owned since it cost fifty-nine Singapore dollars. AND above all else, it was a birthday gift from his parents and also for having passed his PSLE even though he had passed without much flying colors!!! His watch had served him well for the past three years and it had already held such sentimental value for Dave so imagine his incense when he realized it had stopped working altogether!

"Look at what you did to my cherished watch! It's my one and *only* prized possession in the whole wide entire world! Did you guys have to..."

But before Dave could finish his sentence, a big strong brown hand had reached out to grab him by his right shoulder.

"Cool down my prince," growled Musscus in his coarse and low voice, "It is apparent you have absolutely no idea of what's going on. Yet this I can assure you of."

With a very serious expression now on his hairy face, the Dog-man looked Dave straight in the eye, knelt suddenly in front of the disorientated teenaged boy, as did Hootus, and continued calmly.

"No, this is no joke. We are for real and *these* certainly are *not* costumes we are wearing. They are our everyday attire. You are no longer in the land where you grew up as a commoner and no, you were nary abducted, though in a sort of way, you were...spirited away. Fact is, you have been, well, literally summoned home; to the kingdom you were born in and yes, you ARE a prince of royal blood by noble birthright!"

"Oh, and do forgive us, your Highness, where are our manners! Allow me to formally introduce ourselves."

With a low bow, "I am Musscus Del Ellucardes, a royal palace guard and a member of the Seven Secret Elite Guardians of *Phantasy*, or S.S.E.G.P. for short. This weirdo standing next to me has been my childhood companion and best friend for ages and unfortunately, more (years) to come, I'm certain of that."

Hootus was about to open his trap again in resentment to what Musscus had just said but was halted by a timely huge hairy black paw to his fragmented face.

"As I was saying, your Highness," Musscus was now staring with an unearthly and resolute intent into Dave's eyes, the air around him seemingly coming to life with an electric charge Dave had never seen or felt before in all fifteen years of his young life.

"Standing next to me is none other than the great Hootus Von Cress Dermel, head of the three royal stewards serving his Majesty, King Devonus, ruler of the Land of the Beyond, where we now stand."

"We were given new assignments just before you were summoned here... In other words, we are now your very own personal bodyguard and butler...as long as you're here, and we're with you, my young prince. In short, we," Musscus paused and pointed proudly to both Hootus and himself, "serve you now."

"Wait a minute. Did he just say the Land of the Beyond? That sounds familiar," thought Dave. Now where had he heard that mentioned before he wondered.

Hootus only nodded his head in enthusiasm as he beamed teary-eyed with pride at Dave. But all that came out of Dave's mouth was a simple "Huh?" as the poor lost teenaged boy tried his best to digest the information Musscus had just fed him. None of what the Dog-man had just announced made any sense to Dave.

With a weary sigh, Musscus stepped closer to Dave and placed both his hands on the young commoner prince's shoulders.

"Look, Prince Dave. I know you're confused and all but that's only natural. It's one of the many reasons we are here at your assistance, alright? There is someone you have to meet who will explain everything and answer all the questions in your head and we are going to bring you to him now. But before we do that, I have a question for you and you have to answer me truthfully, aye? Take your time to think before you answer."

A vision of Uncle Jones suddenly came into Dave's mind and instantly, he felt at ease and everything seemed to be fine again. He started to breathe easier and the helplessness he felt within his heart melted away. A smile even formed on his face as Dave recounted the happy times he had with Uncle Jones.

"Do you believe in...*magic?*"

This simple yet crucial question caught Dave by surprise. It was not exactly the type of question he had anticipated but at the same time, he gave it some serious thought. Dave closed his eyes and started to recall all the fairy tales and fantasy stories he had read so far. There was magic in them. Then he tried to relate everything he had encountered so far in this strange land that was new to him yet felt so strangely familiar, as if he belonged to it and was a part of it all, one way or another even though he had never stepped foot on the land he now stood on. That was when the answer hit him.

The expression on Dave's face was now one full of confidence instead of confusion that lingered seconds ago. For the very first time in his young life, Dave felt he had total control over his own life, feeling the raw power surging from within his body that rightfully belonged to him, even though it lasted but a mere few seconds. He had no idea what the future held for him, regardless of his status as a prince or commoner, but he felt prepared and ready to face whatever obstacles were to come his way. Or so he thought.

Dave nodded his head slowly and deliberately once. "Yes," was his silent reply and he meant it with all his heart.

The next thing Dave knew, he wasn't in an open grass field anymore.

He was now truly in *Phantasy*, the Land of the Beyond, the mystical and magical fairy-tale kingdom he was born in but never knew existed, until now.

"Great!" exclaimed an egg-cited Hootus who had remained silent whilst his good friend did the ice-breaking and all. The Egg-man could hardly contain his excitement at all the events that were to unfold soon. First of all, there was going to be a father and son reunion in a while and not just any ordinary father and son reunion, mind you, but that of a mighty king and his 'abandoned' son whom he had not set his eyes on for the last fifteen years since he was a baby. Who knew what was going to happen next at the rate things were unfolding in *Phantasy*, an age-old mystical kingdom with a history not many knew of, filled with magic and fantasy where anything impossible is nothing more than a myth! Where anything possible is...well, nothing more than a daily chore!

But first...

"We're on the first (baby) step of your journey home, my young courageous prince! We are going to bring you to meet your one and only real kin in this entire universe whom you have never, err, met before...oops, perhaps I may have said too much already!"

Musscus sighed, shook his head and mumbled, "As usual, Hootus, as usual."

"Well, okay...let's go then!" said Dave who was very curious indeed to find out what was to ensue next.

Thus, that was how the young and mentally-challenged teenaged loser's life changed drastically when he had turned fifteen. Dave had gone from zero to hero, with a generous helping of ups and downs along the way. And oh, let's forget not some new acquaintances along the way as well, both good and bad.

(This concludes Chapter 5.)

CHAPTER 6:

A FIGHTING CHANCE.

Perhaps it was all still too early for Dave to have the adventure of his life. He was, after all, only a mere boy of fifteen who had lead a most normal and monotonous life indeed under the fierce protective wings of his (foster) parents and not the least prepared at all for whatever laid ahead of him. Dave knew nothing of life other than school and home. Most of the time, his mother would be the one fetching Dave home from school. Rarely was he ever seen walking home alone after school had ended.

Even on the rare occasions that he did, he would be escorted by this huge lone Doberman which never failed to disappear once Dave had reached the safety of his flat's void deck and taken the lift up to the level where his flat was located. It was strange Dave showed no fear toward the black and tan noble-looking dog even during the first time it appeared to accompany him home from school. But then again, Dave had always had a soft spot for animals, big and small, fierce or not! There was this one time Dave took a peek at the expensive-looking collar out of curiosity and engraved on the identification tag was the name 'Musscus'. Dave now understood why he had found his new bodyguard so familiar!

It was only natural Dave had his fair share of fantasies from all the fantasy-fiction story books that he had been exposed to since young and thoroughly enjoyed so far. But they were, no matter what, just make-believe only, created from the minds of other mere mortals. Dave had lead a most sheltered life provided and protected by his foster parents thus far. And then there's *this*, this was the *real* deal! The two new acquaintances Dave had just acquired who were now standing before him beaming with pride and respect were real, so was the solid ground he was standing on, and the crisp fresh country air he was breathing from, among all the other sights, smells and sounds he was currently experiencing.

Then again, Dave wasn't like most other teenagers, or humans even.

There was without much of a doubt that Dave, like most kids around his age, was a bright and curious boy with the never-ending thirst for knowledge as proven by the results of his studies in school. Unfortunately, Dave's attention span had always been on the short end of the stick. He had trouble remembering things, except for the things he was interested in, such as chocolate ice-cream, model and remote-control cars and robot hobby-kits (which he could only stare at and dream about but never afford), Hainanese chicken rice (one of the favorite and famous local delicacies of Singapore) and his all-time favorite fantasy story-books and he was always building castles in the air, his mind constantly separated from his body. Dave was never without that stony, dreamy look about him that others usually misinterpreted as arrogance and indifference (I did mention this part about Dave back in Chapter 3, in case you readers have forgotten already).

In other words, poor Dave was a slow developer who didn't quite understand why those within his age-group and especially, his gender were making this huge fuss over puberty until much, much later. While the rest of his peers were busy playing the dating game and discussing about the birds and the bees, Dave was lost in his own make-believe fantasy world in which he was the only 'real' character. The only thing different about Dave at that age was the fact that his fantasies now included robots and not just any normal robots, mind you, but those that were able to 'shape-shift' or transform and hide their true forms that were 'more than meets the eye'. Yup, he had just discovered Gundam and Transformers at fifteen and was truly fascinated by them and their transforming abilities.

So what made Musscus and Hootus so sure that this dreamy young loser of a lad was indeed the savior of their falling kingdom? They didn't. Instead, they were only merely following the orders of their benevolent and wise ruler and it was never their place to question their sovereign's decisions. To do so would mean capital punishment and even death to their entire families! Fortunately for the both of them, that had yet to happen for their king was just as understanding as he was learned. Besides, they were far too valuable to be disposed of just like that. Their superior skills and intellect made Musscus and Hootus a cut above the rest, despite their appearances. Coincidentally that made the two misfits perfect for the latest quest their distraught king had in mind.

"You can open your eyes now, my young prince," said Musscus.

It lasted only a few fleeting seconds but the feeling Dave felt was like he had been rushed through time and space for an eternity! This tingling sensation throughout his entire body was totally new to him and he wanted more of it! It made him trembled with pure excitement the more Dave thought about it. Maybe he would do it with his eyes wide opened the next time even, who knew what he would witness through the pure fabric of time and space? Maybe even someone dead (and) famous like Elvis Presley!

It was hard to describe what it felt like to be transported from one place to the next in an instant, especially for the very first time! It's one of those types of experiences where you had to be there to understand what it felt like. As for Dave, it was nothing short of good, clean wholesome fun. That pure rush of adrenaline cleared Dave's head of all doubts that he really wasn't dreaming anymore. He felt ready now to face whatever was ahead. But nothing could have prepared him for the reality he would face, not what he have experienced in the past or the fantasy adventure stories that he was already familiar with. After all, as the saying goes, truth IS stranger than fiction, no?

"Err, wait, something's not quite right here, Musscus...Where are we? Isn't it kind of cold all of a sudden?" Hootus was trembling more with fright now than with cold even though the atmosphere around the three figures had turned pretty chilly.

"No idea, my old and slightly befuddled friend. But even a fool can easily guess we're NOT in the vicinity of the royal palace as we're supposed to be," Musscus was thoughtful before he continued.

"I remember my old man telling me tales of ancient ruins and tunnels that run deep beneath the old palace itself when I was but a mere pup but never in my wildest dreams did I imagine I would find myself stuck in them with my best friend and the future king himself!"

"Hmmm, I would sure love to explore further but I guess this is not the best time, now is it, Hootus? And since you're the one who got us into this fine mess, you'd better get us all back to the king's chamber before he starts missing us and gives us one of his long-winded lectures again!"

"Yes, yes, of course," stammered a rather freezing Hootus. Just as he started to mutter the right spell that would bring them to their desired destination, Hootus suddenly paused in the middle of his incantation and asked Musscus in a trembling and frightened small voice, "What's, what's that?" pointing a long shaky bony white finger in a certain direction.

A huge dark shadowy form was approaching in the direction Hootus was pointing and Musscus knew at once it was trouble that was coming for them, ancient trouble, no doubt. Trouble spelled with a capital 'T'. The ground shook and heaved and the temperature around the three frightened figures dropped even further still.

"Protect the young prince at all costs! I'll handle this!" growled Musscus who had his trusty two-handed sword Zepphire always ready at his side to defend and attack when necessary. From the corner of his eye, Musscus could see that his royal ward Prince Dave had fallen unconscious to the ground. Hootus was by his side trying to protect and awaken him as best as he could. But Hootus was no fighter or defender. It was all up to Musscus now.

"No, allow me the honors, Musscus." The voice sounded familiar yet it was not possible!

Standing next to Musscus now was the young Prince Dave, albeit a little different this time. There was a bright energetic aura about him and a serious look in Dave's eyes that Musscus had seen before but couldn't quite recall where and when.

"Fun time, baby! Humph, this will be over in no time, boys!" Even Dave's voice sounded different as his lips parted in a half smile while rushing into battle bare-fisted, as if mocking the towering fifteen feet tall monster that was coming for their blood.

The epic battle was over in less than five minutes and poor Dave was once again lying unconscious next to the great big stinking heap of monster trash that was their adversary not so long ago.

Musscus had no trouble picking Dave up even though he weighed almost a hundred kilos, turned to Hootus and muttered, "I haven't the faintest idea what just happened but we'd better report back to the king ASAP. Besides, I don't want to hang around here any longer in case more of those damn ugly creatures come for our blood!"

A deafening roar could be heard in the distance followed by more bloodcurdling roars in unison right after Musscus had finished his sentence. It was almost as though the creatures had heard and understood what Musscus had said and was issuing a challenge to him right there and then.

Pure fear was all written all over Hootus's face and body as he replied, "Sure, sure thing, Musscus, exactly how I'm feeling right now, bro."

Hootus had never felt so frightened and intimidated before in his life as he continued muttering the portal spell under his breath.

He was sure his life-long partner-in-justice felt the same way too even though the Dog-man stood nonchalantly next to him with the sleeping prince over one broad shoulder snoring heavily away, waiting patiently and silently for the enchantment to be completed.

With that said and done, the three disappeared as swiftly as they had come. But not before a pair of glowing red eyes had been spying on them from afar, snickering to itself as it watched the whole event that had unfolded before its very eyes.

"And that, your majesty, was what happened," Musscus was every inch his serious self as he reported to King Devonus the incident that had transpired way beneath the castle due to Hootus's folly, his eyes following closely each and every of the king's actions and reactions, trying his hardest to search for a sign. What sign? Musscus had no knowledge of. He was just following his gut feeling, that's all.

Unbeknownst to all the four of them, including King Devonus himself, it was none of Hootus fault that his spell went wrong somewhere. It was a deliberate and precise intervention that made sure the three ended up where they were, to fight for their lives with the outcome somewhat unexpected yet accountable from a time long ago. To put it bluntly, it was simply a case of history repeating itself.

"Hmmm, interesting...," King Devonus had been all ears as he listened intently to Musscus relating everything that had taken place, right from the very moment his long disentangled son was brought back to the land that would one day belong to him to rule over, to the very latest event that had just occurred right beneath his fortified home, pacing about his spacious bedroom quietly as he did so.

"Ha, ha, ha!!! But of course, that just proves all the more he's really my flesh and blood! He has the fighting spirit of his ancestors within him alright! And let's not forget *my* blood as well!"

King Devonus was all smiles as he laid his eyes on the still sleeping rotund form on his royal king-sized bed.

There was hope yet.

This 'hope' was now sleeping soundly on his bed and Devonus was extremely proud of it since this 'hope' was his only son who had just defeated a fifteen feet tall monster without any formal training in combat. And probably without his realizing why or how he did it as well.

(This concludes Chapter 6.)

CHAPTER 7:

A FRESH NEW START.

O ver the next few days, Dave's young yet troubled life was rendered upside down by the adverse turn of events and characters he could only find in his wildest dreams (or nightmares) and he was truly exhausted by the seventh day. The Land of the Beyond was no dream or fantasy either and the life of a *real* prince wasn't exactly a bed of roses as he had deemed it to be. Dave felt he had had enough and wanted nothing more to do with *Phantasy* and its inevitable fate. For him, reading and fantasying about fantasy adventures was one thing. But to actually live and breathe in one himself was another thing altogether!

There was no fun training to defeat monsters from dawn to dusk every single day. His whole body ached at the end of each day and Dave felt as if he had already been enlisted for the army, or worse. So whoever said life was a bed of roses as a prince obviously was never one himself! This was a bed of roses all right – a bed of roses filled not with sweet-smelling flowers but thorns instead! Where was the fun and excitement of hunting exotic wild games and evil-doers, the glory and thrill of rescuing damsels-in-distress and most of all, the luxury and lazing around all day doing nothing but ordering his loyal servants about that he had so often read in the fairy-tales? And was there even a beautiful princess-in-distress for him to save from the hands of some evil and twisted sorcerer eventually and marry her, have some beautiful children with her and live happily ever after that? It was all just an illusion! Seriously, what had Dave gotten himself into!

Well, by the end of one week's suffering as a prince with a much too heavy burden on his shoulders, Dave left the Land of the Beyond for good. He was all tears as he hugged the only one true parent he had left; King Devonus, good bye. Dave knew he could not have been the chosen one to save his dying kingdom from its inevitable fate. It was an ill-fated mistake right from the start! If there was indeed a God somewhere out there, He was certainly making a cruel joke out of Dave! In his heart, Dave felt he was nothing more than a fat and clumsy teenaged boy who lacked the courage and strength required to run a kingdom and it wasn't always a bed of roses living the life of a prince.

Dave gave up living the life of a mighty sovereign just like that without a fight and returned to Singapore where he chose to live the remainder of his life as another common civilian with his two poor but contented foster parents without regrets. Nobody knew what happened to Dave after he had presumably finished his studies, matured, started working and how he lead his life after both his foster parents had died. Did Dave ever secretly harbor thoughts of returning to his father and kingdom to seek his forgiveness before the old king died? Did Dave actually returned to *Phantasy* after the demise of his foster parents and ruled over his kingdom as was his original and true destiny? Did he eventually find a good maiden to settle down with? And if he did indeed settle down, how many kids did Dave have? So many questions yet no answer! It was as if the character called Dave had never existed in the first place. He became just another face in the crowd, lost in oblivion....

THE END

Wait, that's it? It's the end already???!!! What a rip off! That was fast, what a really short story...

Gotcha!

Got you readers real good, didn't I?

Of course, that wasn't what really happened to our young and lost hero-to-be. Frankly-speaking, how I wish that was true so the novel can end here and I, the author of this tall-tale and modern-day fantasy adventure, can call it a day. But then again, that wouldn't be fun at all and I bet a lot of you readers out there must be dying to find out what REALLY befell upon Dave next. Fret not for here is the real Chapter 7!

As the story continues...

"Your Majesty, I believe the young prince is finally waking up," observed a keen-eyed Hootus who had been keeping a close watch on Dave ever since their escape from the maze and ruins beneath the palace.

It had been one long and eventful day filled with nothing but trouble and Musscus and Hootus, although both apparently tired, were still nonetheless in King Devonus's private chamber watching over the motionless Prince Dave's figure as he laid soundly asleep snoring loudly away like nobody's business on the king's super-sized bed as they reported to the king the events that had transpired since the young prince's first appearance back home.

"Okay, gentlemen, I think that's quite enough for today! Time now to call it a day and chill at the bar with a cold long one or whatever it is you big boys do to relax at the end of a long, hard day's work. Go! You guys deserve it!" said King Devonus as he winked at the two men he trusted the most in his entire kingdom. "It's time now for a very private father-and-son talk."

Musscus and Hootus bowed deeply and respectfully as they closed the heavy double wooden doors behind them.

"What now, old chap?" asked Hootus as he stared expectantly at his best friend and partner-in-justice.

Musscus shrugged his heavy shoulders with an even heavier sigh. "The usual, what else? It's time to hit the royal bar, so said the king himself! Hey, face it, old friend, there's simply nothing else better than chilling over some iced-cold ale and watching gorgeous babes strut their stuff while waiting for further instructions from his majesty."

"True that, true that," nodded Hootus with a silly grin as they both made their way to the royal bar, arms around each other's shoulders as a sign of their close friendship.

"Or we could simply hit the sack. It's been a long, long day so far and I'm hopelessly tired from all that running and fighting."

"What fighting?" teased Musscus as he stared blankly at Hootus and pretended he had no idea what the Egg-man was talking about.

Back in King Devonus's bedroom, an exhausted figure was just starting to stir on the royal king-sized water bed.

"What...where...where am...I?"

"Hush now, my child, you're safe for now," being the wise and learned man that he was, King Devonus could see the confusion in the young prince's eyes.

"Relax, Dave, you're home already, back where you truly belong. Everything's going to be all right, my son. I'm so happy you have finally returned to my side."

"Huh? What, really...? How...do you know my name? Oh...I remember now...I think."

An awkward pause ensued with both father and son staring at each other followed by another pause later...

"Wait, who are you again?"

"You know, I find you kind of familiar but I just can't remember right now...my head hurts and your scent...I think I've smelled it in school before," Dave exclaimed weakly before dropping back into deep sleep again.

Devonus could only stare helplessly with a resigned look on his face at the stationary figure lying on his bed (again...) as he shook his handsome head and thought to himself, "You are not making this easy for all of us, my son."

(This concludes Chapter 7.)

CHAPTER 8:

WHAT WRONG IMPRESSIONS!

Ten very long and exhausting days had flown by since Dave had learned the truth about his mysterious past and background. It had never ever before crossed his mind that he was prince and heir to a mystical kingdom that he had never heard of or been to until the fateful day he was, as those two had put it, 'summoned' without his consent home not long after he had turned fifteen. Dave couldn't understand what all the fuss was about really. He was after all, just the average simple boy living a simple and poor life with his foster parents.

Just like every other normal person, Dave couldn't believe his luck and relished the thought that he was actually of noble birth. Had he hit the mother of all lodes? The blood that was coursing through his body was of the royal ilk and not normal like most people. Still, blood was, simply, blood. It was red in color, royal or not and smelled just like rusted iron, so Dave figured. At the same time Dave did not enjoy the idea nor did he understand the concept behind training hard every single day in magic and physical fitness just to defeat an old nefarious sorcerer or magician or warlock or whatever that he was.

Within the very first day that he had been introduced in the fortified palace of the Land of the Beyond as the true and only crown prince and lone heir to the throne of *Phantasy*, Dave had heard, no doubt, very confidential and private rumors from some of the servants in the palace that the so-called monster he was destined to destroy was ancient and went about his business with the help of a walking stick almost as aged and crooked as the owner himself was. So really, what *exactly* was there to fear from this old man? In Dave's young and naive mind, the young prince imagined that this dark and wicked conjurer was probably no more a threat to the kingdom than the farts he produced and the air he breathed in and the land he traveled on.

By a twist of unlucky fate, or rather, more a blessing in disguise than luck or fate really, word had reached the king's ears soon enough about the young prince Dave's...incorrect impression of the kingdom's greatest threat to its well-being. And so, without further ado, the young misguided prince was summoned promptly to the king's private chambers once again where he would be duly educated before any...well, disastrous results occurred due to Dave's own folly. Devonus knew only too well that challenging Secondras now without any preparation would only mean certain death, or worse!!! But did Dave know that?

"Dave! Who has been feeding your head with all these recent poisonous lies!!???!! You have been back for less than a fortnight and already..."

King Devonus was furious as he demanded from the trembling young prince who had absolutely no clue what was going on now. Why had his father, the great and gracious King Devonus, ruler of a prosperous and flourishing kingdom, who had always been so nice and gentle to him and who had never lost his temper in front of Dave before, become another man altogether without warning? More importantly, what had he done to cause such strong and heated emotions to arise from his father?

Prince Dave could not help but only stand clueless with his mouth much agape and his mind a total blank in front of his angry father. He had no answer and knew not what to say this time.

After a long silence with his head bowed low and eyes on the thickly carpeted floor, one word did escape Dave's mouth.

It was a feeble and almost inaudible "Sorry."

Dave felt like he was back in school being punished by one of the many teachers who hated him for all the wrong reasons. Hot tears were now streaming down his flabby cheeks. All his life Dave had felt alone and miserable with everybody around him never understanding him or at least not making the slightest effort to. And now even his own father whom he had finally just met after so many years of separation was treating him the same way everyone else did. Even his foster parents whom he had lived with for the last fifteen years of Dave's young life did the same sometimes. Enough was enough!

Dave turned and was about to run out of the huge posh bedroom when a tall and warm fuzzy object blocked his way. The young prince looked up and was not the least surprised to find Musscus in his way as usual.

"Prince Dave..."

"That's okay, Musscus, thanks for the help. I'll take over from here," King Devonus was back to his usual calm and collected self as he walked slowly with deliberation over to where Dave was still sobbing quietly and placed a hand on his shoulder.

"Yes, your majesty," Musscus bowed low with absolute respect for his king and closed the double heavy wooden doors behind him.

King Devonus sighed wearily, pulled a heavy ornamented gold chair next to Dave and signaled for him to sit.

"What were you thinking, Dave!"

There was this genuinely worried look on Devonus's face only a father could produce as he continued, "Do you have a death wish or something?"

"Have you no idea how dangerous and evil that twisted old fox is??!!!"

The aging king drew in a deep breath, exhaled and placed both hands on Dave's fleshy shoulders. King Devonus's first intention was to hug his son but then thought the better of it. His voice had that soft and soothing effect on Prince's Dave confused mind as the king carried on with his lecture.

Thus began the lengthy and much needed lesson on the nemesis that was Secondras the most fouled creature that ever lived, breathed and walked, courtesy of King Devonus, ruler of *Phantasy*, Land of the Beyond. By the end of it, Prince Dave had become very much enlightened and he no longer thought of Secondras the Warlock as a mere helpless weak old man who required the aid of an equally old and smelly walking stick to move around.

As a matter of fact, that ancient and smelly piece of 'walking stick' was a very powerful wand indeed with a deep, dark history of its own. It even had a name which could not be uttered. Secondras drew most of his ominous power from it, as well as from the various little other accessories he wore on his bony and deceptively 'weak' body and now, to Dave, Secondras the nefarious Warlock wasn't merely just a nothing and a smelly piece of old shit, he had become the young prince's latest and greatest terror and nightmare of them all!!!

Oh noes, what's next! What will happen to the fate of *Phantasy* when it has been revealed that its savior has turned out to be nothing more than a young and fat useless teenaged prince no older than fifteen who pissed easily in his pants and fainted without obvious help at the slightest hint of danger!

(This concludes Chapter 8.)

CHAPTER 9:

MIGHTIEST WEAPON OF THEM ALL.

Since time unknown, mankind and beasts alike have had many worries to content with in order to survive from one day to the next. As mankind evolved, so did his methods of survival, as well as his surroundings, and rivals. To survive and stand above the rest, he knew he had to be better, smarter, faster, stronger, fitter and most of all, bigger and more ruthless than the rest of his competitors.

That was basically how the land of *Phantasy* came about and how its first rulers emerged and evolved. Sadly, most records of its history from that era have been lost with time through the countless wars and battles it had witnessed and gone through. One king of history past did finally managed to unite the whole of the Land of the Beyond as one kingdom and his name was King Ludenmus Fea Cotuus, Dave's great, great, great, great, great, great, great, great grandfather (whew!). He was known as the father and founder of *Phantasy*.

Before that, the Land of the Beyond was ruled by many smaller rival clans forever at war with each other. It was a life's worth of effort to conquer all the other competing tribes. Countless lives were lost and sacrificed doing so but such was the price of war. Unfortunately for King Ludenmus, by accomplishing such a great deed whereby no other king or ruler had done before him, the entire lineage of this particular king had doomed itself. For without his knowledge, King Ludenmus had made one very powerful enemy along the way of doing what he thought was the only right thing to do.

It was just days before King Ludenmus had eventually merge the entire kingdom of *Phantasy*. He had but only one more rival clan to defeat and conquer before he could unite the whole kingdom as one. After a considerable and exerting battle which lasted for many weeks, both rulers were down to their last few soldiers and ultimately, the two leaders themselves. It was an epic battle which lasted a few more days before King Ludenmus managed to slice off the head of his antagonist cleanly from his neck with one fell swoop of his sword. Yet before his final breath, his enemy muttered a curse that made sure the reign of King Ludenmus and his descendants would last for no more than eleven generations before the kingdom would fall apart and slowly but surely fade and disappear into nothing.

Coincidentally, that adversary who died by King Ludenmus sword was none other than Secondras's father. Ever since he was a youth, Secondras had vowed vengeance on King Ludenmus and his lineage. His father had been a powerful sorcerer who was able to summon and control demons and other minions from the depths of hell. Secondras's father's dark magic and influence over hell was so potent that he was able to return to the world of the living via his son's dreams to school him in the evil arts of the occult so that one day, his son would be able to avenge his untimely death. And now, ten generations of the Fea Cotuus after his father's passing, the time for vengeance had finally arrived, MUAHAHAHA!!! It was time to end everything once and for all and the more Secondras thought about it, the more he couldn't wait for the day he would get to end Davy Fea Cotuus's life there and then just had his great grandfather had done to Secondras's poor father aeon ago. As for the last of the Fea Cotuus's soul after his death, he had other plans for it.

For almost a millennium had Secondras the Warlock waited patiently to seek revenge on behalf of his father. No mere mortal was able to survive that long and even if he did, he would have become so bored somewhere along the way he would have gone crazy already! Not Secondras though, certainly not him. He was always up to some mischief somewhere and knew exactly how to keep himself entertained constantly in his own dark and perverted ways. So how did Secondras do it? What was his secret to longevity, or rather, immortality even? Many great and powerful leaders and rulers alike (mainly from the past) have tried in their own different and unique ways (which usually involved sacrificing lives of the innocent and spilling their blood) and fortunately for us, none had succeeded so far. Can anyone imagine how our lives would be like today if they did???!!!

Believe it or not, Secondras started out his life in a very normal way just like everyone else. He was never born evil to start with. That only happened in the movies and books and stories meant to scare little children into behaving themselves by their elders. Secondras lost his mother not long after his birth and was brought up by his nanny. He never saw much of his father for he was a very busy man often away for long periods on his so-called 'field trips'. Secondras's father was, after all, mighty leader of his tribe and the most important man whom every man, woman and child looked up to in his entire community. Even the simple animals knew better than to stand in his way. Secondras hardly knew his own father as a child. But once he had reached the ripe old age of fifteen, he was suddenly enlisted as general into his father's sizable army and trained relentlessly day and night with only one purpose: to conquer and kill the enemy.

As he grew older and attained adulthood, Secondras had become a changed man altogether, and a full-fledged killing machine. He had proven that he was indeed the prodigy of his father and became his (father's) one and only pride and joy. Secondras started to enjoy attacking, plundering, killing innocent villagers, setting their villages on fire and most of all, taking no prisoners as a ruthless adult. There was no love in his heart, not even for his own people. To him, the weak and useless did not deserve to live. Secondras ended up as a tyrant even to his own clan and if not for the support of his equally cruel but tactful father who was skillful with words and always knew what to say, he would have long been exiled from his own tribe!

Secondras's father had taught him all he knew about dark sorcery and more, even after his death, which was the only thing in life Secondras was truly grateful for. He felt indebted to his father which only made him all the more determined to avenge his demise by the hands of King Ludenmus Fea Cotuus. For that act alone, Secondras had vowed he would carry out his father's last wish and made sure the reign of the Fea Cotuus lasted no more than the eleventh king after King Ludenmus. But most of, Secondras had added a most foul and evil curse of his own to his father's just to make doubly sure the Fea Cotuus would be truly no more in existence. If Secondras and his father couldn't rule over *Phantasy*, they made sure nobody else could! How's that for evil! What about Secondras's curse? Why, it was none other than our hero and main character, Dave himself, of course!

Dave was doomed from the start. No one knew that fact other than Secondras himself. Dave was, after all, quite the total opposite of Secondras. In other words, Dave the prince was nothing more than an idiot to Secondras. Secondras knew he had won right from the start and nobody was the wiser other than himself. That was the reason Secondras the nefarious Warlock was always feeling cocky. He was always so full of confidence, so full of himself and now we know why! Over the centuries, he had learned to be patient, among countless other things and could literally wait an eternity just to seek revenge.

(This concludes Chapter 9.)

CHAPTER 10:

A RENDEZVOUS OF OLD FRIENDS.

It has been two weeks into the June school holidays by now and Dave was finally running out of excuses to return to the Land of the Beyond. It was pure work and truly exhausting to wake up early in the morning and return late in the evening hot, sweaty, tired and smelly as a pig. Besides, Dave's foster parents weren't exactly stupid. They might be poor and simple folks but they were educated, even if only to a small degree.

A part-time job was the first thing that came to Dave's mind but where would he get the money to show his parents as proof even though it was supposed to be just a few hundred dollars? A month-long camping trip to St. John Island (one of many tiny islands surrounding Singapore that's legally part of the republic) was not a bad idea but that would mean getting an adult to sign for the excursion form and Dave knew none of his foster parents would approve of him even leaving home for just one day and night to stay over at a class-mate's place even for the sake of studying. Dave had actually thought of it all, including getting his real father to sign for the excursion form but then again, what if the principal got suspicious of the signature or his parents got worried and tried to contact one of the teachers supposedly involved in the excursion...

It was horrible, a disaster! Dave really couldn't come up with any good idea any more. He gave up. If only there was some way for his foster parents and real father to meet, then maybe... Wait, of course, that's it! It was so simple! Why hadn't Dave thought of it sooner! It was so simple and yet it had not crossed his mind earlier. Maybe it was due to the fact that it was so real and simple he never gave it any real thought, really.

That settled it. But now how was he going to get them to meet? Dave simply couldn't just invite King Devonus to his humble 3-room flat casually and expect the three adults to hit it off just like that! Or could he? What Dave hadn't counted on was the fact that King Devonus and the Teos knew each other from long ago. Or why would the king have entrusted baby Prince Dave in their hands? Dave was trembling with excitement at the idea. He couldn't sleep the night before he was to execute his simple yet brilliant plan. All he had to do was to casually bring up the subject of his home in Singapore and how it would be so delightful that his foster parents back in Singapore would love to meet a real king from another world, who was in fact, Dave's real father!

Well, that opportunity came soon enough and things went as the young prince had initially planned.

It was the end of yet another day of studying the history of *Phantasy*, the different types of magic and their various uses and physical education such as sword-training and horse riding which coincidentally, were very much like what Dave was going through in school back in the other world. Except the subjects he studied there were pretty tame and lame and boring unlike what he was going through in the Land of the Beyond!

Prince Dave was chilling in King Devonus's private chamber that was understandably restricted to only members of his royal family and those he trusted with his life such as Musscus and Hootus. It was not the crown prince's regular habit to stay back this late in the mystical kingdom that was his to rule one day due to his over protective foster parents back home in Singapore. But today was special and tonight was the night he was going to carry out his 'fool-proof' plan of bringing his foster parents and real father together who he presumed had never met before in their lives. Boy, was *he* going to be the one truly surprised!

"Hey, Dada, guess what?"

A curt "What?" was the only response Dave got from King Devonus as the king continued burying his big nose in the thick books he seemed to enjoy reading, not that he really wanted to. It was part of the young prince's father's job as king to know as much as possible and find solutions to the endless problems his subjects face every day, especially the less common ones.

"You know, I have been here in *Phantasy* for quite a while now and it's only fair how I wish *you* could go back to Singapore with me sometimes to visit the tiny flat I stay in with my foster parents. It is such a stark contrast compared to this enormous magnificent palace with its variety of impossibly different functional and colorful rooms! It's just like a fancy 10-star hotel, only bigger and better in more ways than one!"

(Looking around his father's huge luxurious 10-star bedroom) "You know, now that I think about it, your bedroom is way bigger than even the whole 3-room flat we (meaning Dave and his foster parents) stay in! I was just wondering, exactly how many rooms are there in the palace, Dada?"

"Ten thousand," was the nonchalant reply from his father, King Devonus.

Dave almost choked on his own breath when he heard the answer. "Wow..." was all that he managed to say until the dreamy crown prince thought how wonderful it would be to explore each and every room, to which the king answered with a firm "Impossible".

"But why, I'm your son, the crown prince and rightful heir to this magical land and everything in it! Or so you claimed!" Prince

Dave was pouting as he sulked like a baby whose favorite toy was taken from him for not behaving himself, sans the crying.

To which the wise and patient king explained that certain rooms in the royal palace were accessible only to the king himself and no one else. And since Dave was just a prince and was not king, not yet anyway, he was not qualified to enter those rooms specifically restricted only to the king of *Phantasy.*

"So, what's so special about them? Why so secretive, Dada?" asked a very curious Prince (only) Dave.

To which King Devonus told his son he would find out only when the prince himself was king one day. This made Dave sulk and pout his lips even more. Why did he get the sinking feeling they were going round in circles?

After about five minutes of silence while both father and son were lost in their own thoughts, the curious crown prince glanced at his prized Casio watch and suddenly remembered the actual reason he had stayed back so late after his princely daily training. Oh boy, was he going to get it from his foster parents later! Unless...

"Dada, err, as I was saying earlier, I think you should come meet my foster parents back in Singapore, you know. They are really nice and cool people (yeah, right, coming out from the mouth of a loser) so you should really meet them, Dada! Singapore is sooooooo unlike this kingdom that's more old country than modern city compared to Singapore. A change in environment can sometimes be a good thing you know?"

There was a twinkling in the aging king's eyes as never seen before by his son after Dave's calculated speech.

The gears in King's Devonus's head were starting to turn furiously again. "Why not, that's it! You're a genius, my son!" thought the king.

Something big was forming in the middle-aged king's head as he stared wondrously at Crown Prince Dave, his son. He had been so busy being involved in his country's prosperity and daily mundane affairs and problems that he had cleanly forgotten all about the people he had entrusted his son's young life to in the first place; the Teos! Yes, the time had come to meet them and discuss the young prince Dave's future. It was now Devonus's turn to tremble with excitement as a bewildered Dave looked on at his aging and slightly pot-bellied father who had stood up suddenly and was now doing a little funny dance of his own. Score!

After some preparations and with the mumbling of a few magical words and the wink of an eye, both regal father and son were instantly transported to the void deck of the block of flats somewhere in Chai Chee where Dave stayed with the Teos.

"So this is where you have been living all the time you were in Singapore?" asked an astounded King Devonus who was now dressed in modern casual clothes to blend in with the modern crowd of Singapore, so to speak, as he glanced about his new unfamiliar surroundings with an incredible expression which Dave misunderstood for curiosity and amazement. The king was playing along, of course. They were now waiting for the lift to bring them up to the level where Dave and his foster parents lived. In Devonus's mind though, he was thinking, "Wow, this place has sure gone through a lot of changes since the last time I was here. I can hardly recognize this place at all! I can't even remember when the last time I was here was! Damn, has it been *that* long already?"

Dave was trying his best to impress his father and be the courteous host at the same time as he introduced the different parts of the block of flats where he stayed with his foster parents while waiting for the old and inert lift to make its way down from the tenth floor at its own leisurely pace. "At least some things haven't changed," King Devonus couldn't help but chuckle secretly.

Even now Dave hadn't realized who had put him at the doorsteps of the Teos in the very first place when he was still but a tiny little baby. If only he had given it some thought!

A peculiar silence occurred between both father and son when they were in the lift. Maybe it was because there was someone else in there with them along the way up. An old Indian lady holding precariously onto an equally worn-out and bent walking stick like her life depended very much on it who smelled very funny like she had not bathed for many weeks or months or years even had joined them at the very last few seconds just as the lift door was about to close.

Dave assumed she was one of the many neighbors living in the same block of flats as he did even though he was positive he had never seen her before. She got off at the sixth floor while they continued ascending to the eleventh storey where Dave lived. The old Indian lady turned her head back while the rest of her body was facing forward and gave the both of them a crooked grin which revealed many yellowed sharp fangs as the lift door closed behind her. As usual, Dave hadn't noticed anything unusual about that strange old lady other than her offensive body odor but his father sure did. That foul smell was very familiar and before he could reach a conclusion, the lift door had opened again.

A puzzled Devonus stopped Dave in his steps before they had reached his flat. "Don't you live *here*?" asked his father, pointing to the two-room unit Dave and his foster parents used to live in before they shifted.

"No, Dada, not anymore. We shifted to the corner flat five years ago because it's bigger with an extra room for me..."

Dave voice trailed to a halt as the truth hit him.

"Wait a minute!!! How, how did you know where I used to live?" asked a stunned Dave as he stared stupidly at Devonus. "I... don't remember telling you that or anything else about my personal life in Singapore, not even in school! All we discussed about were my homework, my troubles and problems in school and dreams..."

The young prince had gotten cautious and was searching for something to use as a weapon against his own father. He had learned a thing or two after all. Still, Dave had a long way to go!

"And about magic and fantasy and how you wished you were a prince or a knight in shining armor and not a commoner so you could escape from it all."

A sigh could be heard from the older man.

"Yes, how can I forget that part, Dave? The only reason I came to the school disguised as a janitor was because I couldn't stand watching you being bullied by your fellow students, your teachers and even that wussy of a man who is your school principal year after year! Dave, remember that you ARE a real prince now. Cheer up, will you. And no, you didn't, son. Now think, Dave, think! Who did you imagine put you at the doorsteps of the Teos all those years long ago? If I hadn't done that, you would surely be dead by now!" King Devonus laughed heartily as he clasped Dave's right shoulder firmly.

All that commotion had not gone unnoticed. A door opened and two curious and concerned heads poked out and some gasps could be heard as they recognized the tall, handsome and bearded figure standing outside their house with their (foster) son Dave, albeit with more volume around his mid-section now.

Amidst a few hugs and greetings later, King Devonus was finally invited into the Teos humble tiny three-room flat which actually meant it contained one teeny bedroom next to the slightly larger main or master bedroom plus a small living room followed by an even smaller dining cum kitchen area in the back of the flat complete with just one small cubicle as a toilet/bathroom. It was indeed a tiny flat big enough for a family of three or four to fit in. Otherwise, it would have been too cramped with all that squeezing everywhere.

Both Michael and Michelle Teo were very surprised and curious indeed to find King Devonus with their (fost...oh, never mind, it should be understood by now) son Dave. A million and one questions were flowing through the couple's heads as the four of them sat on the floor of the almost sparse living room which normally would be occupied by a few sofas, a table or two, some standing fans, a huge television set and a fancy house phone as was the standard in most other living rooms. But in the Teos' version, there were only a small broken and chipped coffee table complete with a cheap-looking plastic house phone on top which resembled more of a toy rather than an actual functioning house phone. Other than that, it was a spacious and clean living room really due to the lack of furniture.

"My, oh my, how long has it been since we last met, your Majesty?" It was more a statement than a question that came out of Michael Teo's mouth. "Let's see now, about seventeenth years, hasn't it? Unless my memory fails me, which, unfortunately for *you*, it hasn't," Michael grinned as he sat facing the king.

"Where the hell have you been, old friend, we missed you!" said Dave's foster father as he punched Devonus playfully in the arm.

"Really, has it, Mikey? I can't remember, sorry, my old friend. Been too busy running a kingdom after the death of my own Dada for anything else," Devonus was solemn as he recalled his father, King Otellus, and his last words.

"Yes, we missed you indeed, Devonus. How have you been? The last we heard about you, you were happily married and even had a baby boy not long after. How are the queen and prince?" inquired Michelle Teo innocently.

"Well, about that..." King Devonus suddenly broke down and cried shamelessly in front of the three at the mention of his deceased Queen Katrina.

"Sorry... (sob-sob) for the... (more sob-sobs) sudden display of... unmanly (final sob) emotion," King Devonus apologized as he dried his tears in between sobs.

King Devonus did a series of deep controlled breathings as he calmed himself down before continuing.

"Queen Katrina, my beloved and long dead wife, died not long after giving birth to Dave here (pointing to his son beside him) and I miss her very much, still. We were so in love and were the happiest couple lost in our own blissful world, until Dave came along and destroyed our world together. Sorry, son, I'm just telling the truth here, even if it hurts. Anyway, after my Katrina died I made a pact with the devious devil, aka, Secondras the Warlock. I would surrender my newborn crown prince to him for the return of my beloved Katrina. I know, what was I thinking then, right? But I'm just a man too, you know. I have my weak moments as well, even as a king...sorry. Thing was, I finally woke up my ideas just before I was supposed to hand over baby Dave to the evil warlock."

The king was excited as he continued.

"Remember that little parcel of joy you found at your doorsteps fifteen years back?"

The Teos nodded their heads in unison.

"Well, yes, that was my doing," admitted the king triumphantly.

All this while though, young Dave had been listening with the most incredible expression on his face. He knew better than to interrupt the adults while they were talking. Never in his wildest dreams could he have imagined that his foster parents and real father had met even before he was born!

Thus began a long story-telling session of the infamous warlock and his prophecies and something about seeking the Teos' help when the time came which lasted around two hours and by that time the young prince had already fallen asleep, apparently tired out after a long hard day of princely training and torture listening to a story he was involved in and already knew, well, most of it anyway.

"I'm sorry to have kept all of these from you two but it was for the better I can assure you both!" Devonus sounded apologetic and somewhat a little embarrassed as he said this.

"That's okay," Michael Teo nodded calmly. "More importantly, old friend, what plans do you have for Dave now?"

"I see. So our Dave is actually a prince from a mystical land from beyond and he's been training hard during the school holidays to defeat an ancient arch enemy of your kingdom? Wow, I find that almost impossible to believe if you hadn't told us yourself, your Majesty!" exclaimed an astonished Michelle Teo who still couldn't believe that the boy she had taken care of and brought up dutifully as if he was her own son over the last fifteen years had turned out to be something more than an ordinary abandoned baby who had, sadly, lost his birth mother not long after he was conceived.

In her mind, Michelle was happy she had done a good job as a foster mother so far but she was sad at the same time as something in her heart told her Dave would be leaving them soon to live with his real father, King Devonus in a place far, far away and very unlike Singapore. Oh no, didn't that mean she and her husband Michael were going to be lonely again? Still, what was there for her to do? Which parent and child would want to be separated from each other? She knew she wouldn't, and she would prove it, if only she had one of her own...

"Actually, I haven't really given much thought to Dave's future just yet, considering that he is the crown prince and heir to the kingdom he was born to."

"Of course he will have to return and accept his true destiny as rightful ruler of his kingdom once he turns 21. But for now, I believe he still has school to attend to like every other child his age here in Singapore and I think it's only fair that he stays with you two until he's ready to go home and accept his destiny once and for all!" smiled Devonus.

"My only request for now, though," the king continued with a grave look on his partially wrinkled yet charming face, "is that he be allowed to return home every now and then during the weekends or after school even, if you know what I mean," winked the king unabashedly at the Teos.

"But, of course, your Majesty! How can we say no to a king's request?" Michael Teo said with a tease in his voice. "Surely we commoners would not wish for our heads to be separated from our bodies or hung high atop wooden poles like ragged dolls for all to see, do we?"

"Stop it!" the king laughed, obviously enjoying the jokes Michael was cracking at his expense.

"Well, that settles it then!" said King Devonus as he stood up and stretched his tired long legs.

As he waved his goodbye to the Teos, a light bulb suddenly lit up above Devonus's head.

"Hey, why not you two come visit me back in the ole kingdom sometimes as well!" the king was almost jumping up and down with excitement even at his age.

"We can go fishing and hunting, you and I, Mikey old boy! As for you, Michelle, sweet and lovely always as I remembered, you can dress up in all the finery of a noble, mingle with the rest of the ladies or go horse riding even as I clearly recollect, was one of your favorite hobbies back in the good old days when we were younger, eh!"

Both the Teos stared at each other with a funny look, grinned at Devonus and said "Okay!" together.

(This concludes Chapter 10.)

Chapter 11:

THE DELICIOUSLY ENCHANTING BAIT.

Hidden in a forgotten corner of *Phantasy*, surrounded by a mysterious smoking black fog that never went away, somewhere deep, deep within the heart of a dark and creepy forest known only as the Dark Forest that was reputed to be heavily haunted not just by ordinary ghosts and spirits but demons, zombies, ghouls, ogres, orcs and all sorts of monsters imaginable and unimaginable as well, sat a lonely dilapidated two-storey mansion that appeared to have been abandoned forever and rumored to be inhabited by an evil witch who survived an execution of fire long, long ago.

Legend had it that many brave warriors and adventurers alike had ventured into this mansion but few had lived to tell their tales. The lucky few who did survive however, either lost their minds and were never heard of again or mentioned sights and sounds so creepy and horrible they were more of a living nightmare and scarier than anything else they have ever experienced in their entire lives!

Spooky as it might have seemed, that was not the most interesting part about the creepy mansion in the creepy forest. The abandoned mansion with the supposedly undead witch residing in it was actually nothing more than a front for what was underneath it that was the main focus of everything creepy and unthinkable.

Most people and even animals stayed away from the Dark Forest and the mansion with the man-eating witch in it due to its delightful (yes, that's right, that's the way I like it) frightfully repulsive reputation started many moons ago by none other than Secondras himself, of course. Who else would have the brains, and not to mention, motive besides him? Secondras needed a place to stay after his father had lost the battle to keep his clan and his own people were finally free to turn against him. The young warlock had found the forest by chance one fateful day while running away from his pursuers who, as usual, wanted him dead more than anything else in the whole wide world.

The Dark Forest was not always creepily sinister and home to a whole range of unspeakable horrors that now resided there. It was once a normal rain forest that was home to many wild beasts including monkeys, deer, flying squirrels, humongous snakes with an even bigger appetite, elephants and even a tiger or two. But all that changed the day Secondras the Warlock set foot into the beautiful and tranquil forest while fleeing from his enemies and corrupted everything in it including the wild life. The poor animals that were unlucky enough not to have escaped in time became Secondras's new minions and slaves and were transformed into various different monsters and horrors that existed mainly in nightmares and the depths of hell, their souls lost forever!

As for the so-called forsaken mansion now supposedly taken over by an undead man-consuming witch, Secondras had probably stolen that idea from a fairy tale he had read as a child long, long, long ago called Hansel and Gretel and improvised on it, in his own wicked little ways, naturally.

For many centuries now the nefarious warlock had made the Dark Forest his residence far and away from the hustle and bustle of the kingdom where he could plot his diabolical plans in peace every day without fear of disturbance from intruders many feet underneath the soil which was truly befitting for one as vile a villain such as Secondras himself.

Secondras was seated on his own mock throne he had copied from the actual one from the royal palace (except for the original colors which he had considered were way too bright and shiny for his own liking) and created from the bones of some of his enemies one fine and peaceful dark day, bored and restless as usual. Suddenly his eyes were literally on fire as a new and devious plan began forming in his twisted wicked mind.

"Oh, sweet Petal. Sweet, sweet and dearest Snowpetal. Where is my sweetest and dearest niece with the most poisonous heart and cutest face I have ever known? Come out, come out, wherever you are!" cooed Secondras in his old and broken voice. It was his own unique way of summoning the comely lass he had trained her whole life to be as evil and twisted as he was since she was a toddler. In other words, the one Secondras had just addressed as his niece was going to his successor one day. Not surprising though, *Dave* was meant to be his first choice. But since his arch nemesis had outsmarted him, he had to pick another, didn't he?

Surprisingly, Secondras might have been a hyper villain with a cold heart (or no heart at all) who never batted an eyelid when spilling the blood of his enemies carelessly and indifferently. But he did have a soft side to him after all as was evident here which no one else besides himself, his 'niece' and his closest aides knew about. It was one of his closest guarded secret which Secondras had hoped to bring to his grave someday, *if* he ever died.

"Here I am. It's almost lunchtime, what the hell do you want from me, old man?" a disembodied voice could be heard grumbling beside the old nefarious warlock as a short and stunningly beautiful yet heartless looking girl with skin as white as porcelain appeared from the shadows. She looked no more than fifteen or sixteen and yet there was already a murderous look in her eyes and evil aura about her. Secondras had indeed trained her well, probably too well, which sealed her fate in the end.

"I just had a wonderful thought and I need you to complete and fulfill it for me, my child," smiled Secondras in his own evil and twisted way as he reached out to grab and smell a handful of Snow's long flowing and raven-black locks which had become a habit of his every time she was close to him.

"Mmmm, really, you old faggot? Let's hear it then. I haven't got all day you know," whispered Snowpetal in a soft and seductive voice next to the old warlock's ear.

(This concludes Chapter 11.)

CHAPTER 12:

THE SECRET TRIP, PART 1.

Dave had gotten used to life as a prince by now and things were going well for him in both worlds. Or at least they seemed to be. He had gotten stronger physically although he still maintained his chubby yet cute figure by feasting heartily at the end of each day as prince (this was after the Teos and King Devonus met again). Dave had also grown accustomed to the use of magic which had a tendency to backfire harmlessly on him once in a while causing a laugh or two here and there.

Yet the greatest mystery about him was the different and confidently strong Dave who managed to defeat a fifteen feet tall monster single-handedly and without the aid of any weapons within a matter of minutes when they were misdirected into the ancient ruins and maze deep, deep beneath the royal palace not too long ago.

King Devonus made many attempts at stimulating the same conditions with the help of Musscus and Hootus in order to draw out that other side of Dave. Devonus even constructed a fifteen feet tall robotic machine to fight his son. Alas, the results were all futile which ended with some funny consequences. If only there was a fool-proof way to bring out the fearless side of Dave then the chances of ridding the kingdom of Secondras would be much, much higher.

Unfortunately, that was not the case to be. Which meant the only way to make Prince Dave powerful and wise in the way of magic and swordsmanship was the old-fashioned way. King Devonus hoped that when the time had finally come to face Secondras the evil Warlock, his son would be brave and determined enough to annihilate the old menace once and for all! Or at the very least be an important asset in bring down the ancient terror everyone dreaded. But until then, there was much training left for Dave! His father could see he had become stronger. But for the king, that was not enough and there was room still for improvement! 'Ganbatte' (Japanese word for 'Keep it up') Prince Dave-kun!

Just as his father was obsessed with a stronger son made of meaner stuff, there was something else in Dave's mind that had been bothering him for quite a while now. The young prince had been back in the mystical kingdom that was his true home for three weeks now and all he ever did was to train, train and more training! He was only taught the spell to teleport specifically to the confinements of his own royal bedroom in the royal palace from Singapore and nowhere else in *Phantasy*.

Curiosity soon started to get the better of him and Dave pondered what life outside the palace was like, just as his father did before him and *his* father and those before them when they were still young, curious and full of energy.

Seriously, what was life like in the Land of the Beyond *beyond* the walls of the fortified palace? Prince Dave first thought was to ask his father since he was the king and should know more than anybody else in the kingdom. But then again, the young prince knew for sure that would only most likely end up with him stuck in the palace for a long, long time with nowhere else to go and more training than he could ever handle. Boring! The royal servants and guards and even Musscus and Hootus were nice and loyal to him but they were even more loyal to the king. Who could blame them? Nobody would ever dare disobey and anger their own boss, not especially when that particular boss in question was officially the ruler of their beloved land and home!

Dave's second choice and alternative was...of course, the library! The library was and has always been Dave's favorite hang-out in the entire world, or worlds in his case. That was, until he discovered video console games, portable games and much later, computer games and online gaming. The teenaged prince could not wait to find out what knowledge and secrets he would be able to unearth from all the countless books and secured artefacts from the royal library which also doubled as the royal museum that was opened occasionally not for the eyes of the common man but rather, for the sight of the distinguished noble or rich and influential guests who dropped by the royal palace once in a while. Of course, for Prince Dave, he could enter the royal library/museum as and when he pleased 24/7 and none of the royal guards could either stop or question him.

"So what exactly are we doing here in the royal library and museum and what are we looking for, your Highness?" inquired a rather meddlesome Hootus who was always getting in Dave's way as usual and asking questions that never seemed to end. Musscus, on the other hand, was always cool, polite, hardly spoke and always there to lend a helping hand without being asked to when needed. The Egg-man, however, was always there whether he was needed or not and that was really starting to irritate Prince Dave a lot.

"Nothing really, just thought I'd look around the library and museum since I haven't been here yet," mumbled the rather annoyed crown prince. He kept wondering why Hootus was still awake following him all over the palace when it was clearly late in the night and everyone else was asleep, well, almost everyone else was! Musscus, on the other hand, was always welcomed in his company!

The youthful and immature crown prince was still walking around in circles in the royal library/museum hoping to shake the Egg-man off when he accidentally stumbled into a bookshelf and a dull-looking dusty old book dropped off and fell onto the wooded floor. It was a book about old maps and places of interest to visit in the magical and mysterious fantasy kingdom.

In Dave's mind he was thinking, "Great! Exactly what I'm looking for!" as he quickly picked the book up and hid it in his baggy clothes with one swift motion hoping no one else had noticed. Hootus sure hadn't since he was distracted by the more 'interesting' side of the museum and the strange and mysterious artefacts housed in it. His partner-in-justice, on the other hand, heard and saw what Dave had done but chose to keep his mouth shut and pretended he saw nothing out of the obvious. Musscus hadn't the faintest idea what the young and foolish prince was planning but he knew exactly what to do.

"Hmmm, did he?" asked a very inquisitive King Devonus as Musscus reported to him the incident from the royal library after almost everybody else in the palace had gone to bed, including Hootus the Egg-man.

"And did you see what book he took?"

"Yes, I believe it was an old book about maps and landmarks to visit in our kingdom, my Liege. But it was a rather old and very outdated book the prince took and many of the more interesting places..., as you may already know, have changed over the years and some have even been corrupted by the evil warlock," replied Musscus.

The gears in King Devonus's head were turning and he asked Musscus after a slight pause, "Are you thinking what I'm thinking, my young and furry canine friend?"

There was a deeply perplexed look on the middle-aged king's handsome face as he stared into empty space. What was his son up to this time???!!

"Sire...?"

"I'm afraid this is dire, Musscus. Since he's my own flesh and blood and if I have not guessed wrongly, I'd say he's going to explore *Phantasy* itself!"

"What! We must stop him from such a foolish act, your Majesty!" the dead serious expression on the royal guard's face said it all.

Surprisingly, a hearty laugh escaped from the king's mouth.

"Why stop him? Let him go! This is a great learning opportunity for the young and ignorant crown prince to learn how to survive and defend himself in the real world!" reasoned King Devonus triumphantly.

"He has been cooped up within the safety of the palace and there are many pairs of eyes watching and protecting him all the time and he knows that. He has achieved the purpose of the training I have designed for him so far."

"But," continued the king as he turned and faced his number one and best royal guard and knight in the entire kingdom there was in the eyes with a very serious tone and look on his face now, "I want you and Hootus to be there by his side at all times! Protect him at all costs, including your very lives! Should anything happen to my one and only son who is next in line to the royal throne, you know only too well what will happen to you and your families, don't you?"

Musscus immediately kneeled on both knees before his king with his head bowed low and nodded grimly, understanding the new grave mission entrusted to him and Hootus completely.

Then on a much lighter note, "Oh, and speaking of Hootus, please remind him *not* to open his trap so much and ask less questions. It's driving my sweet innocent baby crazy!"

Musscus could only stare blankly at King Devonus, speechless. Parents these days! Even his usual level-headed king was not spared!

(This concludes Chapter 12.)

CHAPTER 13:

THE SECRET TRIP, PART 2.

It was the last week before the June school holidays was to come to an end and every child age sixteen and below had to return to their boring studies and torturing school life. Not everybody felt that way though, there was actually a handful of students who couldn't wait for school to commence and these were usually the school perfects, class monitors and such well-behaved students who excelled in both their studies and extra-curriculum activities who enjoyed going around their school compounds keeping any eye out for the delinquents and punishing them for their evil deeds and sometimes harmless pranks.

As for our clueless hero Prince Dave, he was still trying hard to figure out an excuse or two to sneak out of the palace grounds and explore the vast contents of the mystical kingdom he was going to inherit one day. Fortunately for him, he need not crack his head any longer as the royal announcement came early one morning that training for the entire week had been cancelled due to some 'sudden unforeseen circumstances'. The young prince was happy with the sudden cancellation of his training for the entire week. He was free to roam the mysterious kingdom as and when he pleased for a whole week before school began again! How cool was that?!! It hadn't crossed his simple mind though what had caused the abrupt halt to his training and neither did he bother to find out or at least ask someone. All he cared about now was the promise of adventure!

Unfortunately for Prince Dave, overcoming the first obstacle was all that had occupied his mind the last few days. He hadn't planned anything beyond that as usual and now he was stuck. Being the young and inexperienced teenager that he was, prince or not, Dave had no idea where and how to proceed next. Luckily for our clueless adolescent of a hero, that was the cue for Hootus and Musscus to step in from out of nowhere to his rescue as if they could read his mind.

Both bodyguard and butler playing babysitter to their young and ignorant crown prince were excellent actors as well, among many other things and roles. They pretended not to know what their hapless prince was up to. It was Hootus who spoke first as usual and after that firm warning from King Devonus, he was now trying his best to open his huge mouth less often. Still, it was a challenge that proved too much for the Egg-man to handle and he almost cracked under the pressure (get it? Egg, cracked=cracked egg?).

"Good morning, your Highness. Shouldn't you be still in bed now that there is no training for this entire week and you're free to do as you please?" Hootus bowed in acknowledgment as he greeted Prince Dave who was acting kind of suspiciously in the royal corridor that leaded to the front gates of the palace.

"Going out for an early morning stroll, my prince? And what's that you're carrying on your back? It looks quite big and heavy, doesn't it? If I hadn't known any better, I'd say you're going on a secret picnic or camping trip of some sort, aye?"

Hootus was enjoying himself shooting away as his partner observed silently at his side, arms crossed over his chest. Musscus had known Hootus most of his life now since they were a small egg and a little pup. Hootus might not be brave nor was he good at fighting and fending off enemies. He might not look the part with his broken image, sharp tongue and all but Hootus was truly the best intel there was in the entire kingdom and the main man to count on for getting out of sticky situations and hot soups, solving mysteries and settling prominent disputes among the highly distinguished. With such talents under his belt, it was no surprise Hootus was appointed not only as the Chief Steward to his majesty King Devonus but was his part-time royal advisor as well (the king was that smart).

Musscus, on the other hand, as his name indicated, was the one with the muscles and fighting prowess. He was trained in the art of self-defense and swordsmanship since the tender age of five (in human years) and had never looked back since. Musscus had come from a long line of royal guard dogs that had evolved over time to the present stage that they had become. Maybe it was due to the mysterious mystical forces of magic that surrounded their kingdom at work. Or maybe someone 'up there' thought it was only fair his family deserved the evolution to help combat evil better since they were fiercely loyal right from the beginning. Who knew for sure? What was apparent though was that the Dog-man was fiercely loyal to the royal family just as his father, grandfather and ancestors were and prepared to protect members of the royal family at all costs including the sacrifice of their lives should the need ever arose.

Both Musscus and Hootus were from the same village and became close friends by chance after the pup-boy had saved the young egg-boy's butt one day from a bunch of no-good bullies out looking for trouble as usual. In the course of time, they grew up together, became the best of playmates, enrolled in the royal services of the royal family once their parents thought the time was ripe for them to, became the best of their classes and line of work, had plenty of admirers and were role models and idols to their juniors and even some seniors.

And now they were both stuck as baby-sitters to this clueless dumbass crown prince they didn't know existed (think along the lines of "Remember what I told you guys years back about me being childless with no heir to the throne? Well, I lied!" and the hopeful candidates' faces that cried or sighed when their only chance to rule their kingdom was ruined and flushed down the toilet) till recently who continued to surprise them as time went by. Maybe, just maybe, there was hope for their doomed kingdom after all?

"So, really, what's up, my Lordship? Are you going somewhere at this early hour of the morning? I smell an adventure in the making, eh, Musscus?" Hootus couldn't stop himself from laughing at his own punt which only he thought was funny.

"Cut it out," Musscus growled. "Can't you see the prince is uncomfortable? Get serious, will you?"

"Oh, I'm sorry, Prince Dave... Here, let me help you with that backpack," offered Hootus as a sign of apology.

"No!" Dave almost shouted as he backed away from the two and searched frantically for a way around them and out of their sight and reach before they could stop him from getting out of the palace and spoiling his plans for the whole week, or at least just for the day. Silly prince, what was he thinking really!

Hootus was about ready to give chase to the running prince when Musscus suddenly placed an arm in front to stop him from going further.

"What the...? Why did you stop me?" Hootus asked his partner-in-justice, confused.

"Let him go," Musscus said as he picked up the book of old maps Dave had dropped in his haste to get away. "He will be back for *this*. Besides, we will be right behind him. He won't be able to go far since he's a stranger in his own land."

Hootus could only stare at his partner with renewed respect. Not only was Musscus strong, he had brains to match his brawns too.

In his mind though, Musscus wasn't sure what the hopeless young prince would do. But it was a risk he was willing to take and a gamble he wasn't about to lose! Musscus was interested to find out what Dave's next move would be and he was sure his prince would be back once he realized that his only source to finding his way around the kingdom had gone missing.

(This concludes Chapter 13.)

CHAPTER 14:

WHAT'S NEXT?

As predicted by his personal bodyguard, Dave hadn't gone far when he realized something important on him had gone missing and was searching everywhere frantically for the book of old maps he had...borrowed without consent from the royal library just the other day.

"Shit! Where is that book of maps I stole, I mean, 'took' from the library yesterday?" thought Prince Dave as panic started to rise within him as he realized he had lost the book of maps he had gone through great lengths to smuggle out of the palace.

Dave searched high and low, in and out of his backpack, even pouring out all the contents inside. He went through his own clothes and all his pockets he had on him but to no avail. Our panicking teenaged hero also traced his way back from where he came from and ceased just outside the palace gates. The rebellious crown prince had no intention of going back into the palace in case someone stopped him from leaving the second time he tried to get out. Now what? Oh wait, could he have dropped the book while escaping from the **DisCriminated Duo** (a nickname he had given his personal royal bodyguard and butler), aka, Musscus and Hootus?

"Is this useless book what you're looking for, my prince?" asked an all too familiar guff voice.

Oh no, Dave's worst fear had come true! He had been discovered and now, all his plans for the entire week and even the weekend and coming Sunday were about to go down the drain. Think, Dave, think!!!

"Huh? What are you talking about?" The teenaged prince's face had gone deathly pale as he slowly backed away and tried to make a run for it from the duo in the opposite direction.

"Wait! You don't have to pretend anymore, your Highness. Neither should you run away from us as if we are the monsters here," Musscus was serious yet laughing heartily by now as he threw the expired book of old maps at Prince Dave.

"Here, catch!"

Being his usual clumsy self, our clueless princely hero failed to turn around and catch the flying object hurled with maybe just a little more force than expected in his direction in time that thus hit him squarely in his face on his right cheek and bounced harmlessly to the ground.

It was such a hilarious sight to behold that Musscus lost all control and was laughing even harder by now, his gangly body bended in half, arms covering his hard and muscular abs whilst tears were flowing without restraint from his eyes. Hootus, who had stood by his best pal without a single word and watching the whole scene unfold before his big round eyes, couldn't take it anymore and joined in the laughter as well.

"Owww! That really hurts! Now my chubby cheek is even chubbier and my face isn't balanced anymore! I blame you for it, Musscus!" grumbled the young prince who stood rubbing his swollen red cheek, more surprised and angry then frightened.

One would have expected Prince Dave to cry by now but strangely enough, quite the opposite happened. As a matter of fact, there was that impetuous bright and sizzling electrifying aura about the crown prince that flashed and disappeared mysteriously. Both Musscus and Hootus instantly recognized it. It was that work of miracle they had both witnessed deep beneath the ancient ruins and maze of the palace the very first time they had brought their crown prince back home.

"Interesting," thought Musscus. Turning to the Egg-man beside him, "Did you see that? It was but only for the briefest moment, yet it actually happened! I wonder why?" The Dog-man made a mental note to report that latest incident to his master when he had the chance to.

Hootus was speechless as he still couldn't believe his eyes. Such raw power, even if it was but for the merest of moments. Wow.

Dave, on the other hand, hadn't the slightest clue what had just transpired. It was the first time he had seen Musscus laugh though, and so much so that he was totally like another (canine) person altogether! Most of the time the Dog-man was just the serious and cool bodyguard with the steely brown eyes and expressionless face who hardly opened his mouth. Dave forgot his anger and fear and sauntered toward his personal bodyguard and butler casually, picking up the book he had stolen...no, borrowed without permission from the royal library along the way. He had come to consider the two his friends after all the time they had spent together.

"What do you mean it's useless?" asked a puzzled Dave as he held up the book of old maps and interesting places to visit in *Phantasy* as close to the face of Musscus as he could. "Explain yourself, quickly!" demanded the prince.

"If you haven't noticed by now, your Highness, there is an expiry date on the last page of the book which clearly states this book has expired many, many decades ago. I bet the head royal librarian has not done his job well enough and either kept missing this book on purpose or has forgotten to dispose of it time after time! I wonder if I should report this to his Majesty? Of course, that would surely mean the head librarian losing his job...and maybe his head even. Nah, a warning should suffice!" was Musscus's lengthy reply.

Before Prince Dave could open his mouth to speak, Musscus continued.

"Besides, have you not noticed the date on the cover itself? This book is now an antique and a very worthless one too! It's more than two centuries old and a lot of changes to our beloved ancient kingdom and famous landmarks have been made since then, no thanks to an evil mad warlock!"

A sigh of relief escaped from Dave after he heard what the Dogman had just mentioned.

"So I didn't steal anything from the royal library after all! Whew, what a relief this is! Which means, of course, I need not explain about 'stealing' this outdated book to my father since it should have been discarded decades ago anyway. In fact, I'm doing everybody a favor by discarding this book now!" a smile spread across the crown prince's silly round face as he thought about what his bodyguard had just explained to him.

"Hold on!" Musscus placed an outstretched huge paw in front of Dave as if he knew about our young princely hero's intention. "I need that expired library book back before we continue, my prince. There is an age-old custom in our kingdom never to dispose of anything from the royal palace outside of its premises, including everyday common rubbish. Besides, I need it as proof against the absentminded head librarian, as well as knock some sense back into that shiny old head of his with it!"

"Are you serious?" asked Dave with an incredulous expression on his face. "How come nobody told me anything about such a weird rule? Are there more such funny laws where this came from?"

Before either his bodyguard or butler could answer him, the young crown prince was already onto another topic.

"Wait! How did you guys know I was going on a secret exploration trip on my own?" Dave kept his guard up even though he knew he could trust those two. After all, they were his father's most trusted sidekicks (I would have preferred to use the word 'minions' here but then again, they were the tried–and-tested good guys) in the entire kingdom. And if his father, king and ruler of the mystical and magical fantasy land they called home, trusted those two jokers with his life, why shouldn't his only son, next in line to be king and all, not trust them? Did that make any sense?

Musscus laughed before explaining. "Two things you need to know, my Lordship. First of all, you are not a proficient liar and neither are you skilled at hiding secrets, even his Majesty knows about it too. Why do you think your training was abruptly cancelled at the last minute? Secondly, you are the *Crown Prince*! You have the right to explore your own kingdom! One day you are going to inherit and rule over this entire land from your father, the king! You do know that, right? You could have told us about your plans earlier and the two of us would have been more than obliged to be your guides as well as protect you along the way, Prince Dave!" a big grin appeared across Musscus's black and brown hairy face displaying his pearly whites for all to see. It sort of scared Dave a little though because they were more like pearly *sharps* than anything else.

"Wow... Sorry, man, I never really thought that much at all. You know me, I'm just a kid. I'm really sorry to have put you guys through all that trouble! If I had given more thought in the first place, none of this would have happened, ha-ha!" Dave laughed sheepishly as he placed one hand behind the back of his head.

All three had a good laugh together and the young and foolish prince was at ease. But the main question remained. Where should he, or rather, they, start exploring first?

"So, guys, any idea where we should go from here?"

(This concludes Chapter 14.)

CHAPTER 15:

AN UNEXPECTED TWIST.

The three stood staring at each other, not sure what their next move would be. There was something Musscus had wanted to inform his young and ignorant royal ward badly and now was as good a time as any.

"Your Highness...there is something you should know about our kingdom," Musscus's voice sounded weak and quite unlike his usual bold and confident self.

"What is it, Musscus? You can tell me. Besides, we are out of the palace and I don't believe anyone else here can hear us talk besides the three of us," reassured Dave.

"That's where you are wrong!" the number one royal guard growled fiercely in defence of the palace he guarded most loyally with his life as his mood changed immediately upon hearing what his truly oblivious young prince had just said. Musscus still could not believe Prince Dave was that purely ignorant of the situation in his own kingdom. Time for some personal education, Musscus's style!

Dave trembled slightly as the tall and muscular palace guard towered over him purposely and snarled menacingly before backing off and apologizing profusely to his confused and frightened prince. Even his long-time childhood friend and companion cowered in fear at the sight of the Dog-man losing his temper. Such was the Doberman's fierce loyalty to his kingdom and palace!

And then it was time for some lengthy explanation.

"We are protected while within the safe confinement of the palace. Unknown to the common folks and even to you, young prince, until now, that is, there is actually a magical force field invisible to the naked eye at work surrounding the entire royal palace and protecting it and all its denizens within from the many real dangers of our mystical kingdom such as straying hungry and ferocious wild beasts, roaming dragons and dinosaurs and most hazardous of all, Secondras's multitude of demonic and undead minions, huge as it is (the palace, that is). Only those truly skilled in the art of magic can see and weaken it."

"But out here! Out here we are truly exposed and vulnerable! We are nothing more than sitting ducks for just about anything! *Phantasy* isn't just your average ordinary magical fairy-tale fantasy kingdom. It has been going through a lot of changes since his Majesty; King Devonus took over as ruler from his father, King Otellus, your grandfather."

"You must understand that your father is a far-sighted genius and completely different from the rest of the previous sovereigns who used to rule this kingdom!"

"He is?" asked the young prince innocently, more immersed in Musscus's story-telling than anything else by now.

"Yes, ever since he took over as king of this land that's full of wonder and mystery, he has implemented numerous changes gradually over the past twenty odd years. Did you memorize at least some of the old maps from that library book you...took the other day, my liege?" inquired Musscus while keeping a sharp eye and ear out for anything out of the ordinary and his hands on the hilt of his trusty and not rusty double-edged sword, Zepphire, an exquisite and formidable gift from the king himself for his ever fierce loyalty to the royal family and never-say-die attitude.

"Yes, yes, of course I did!" answered Dave. "Why do you ask?"

"Now look at this! Do you understand now?" Musscus was slightly concerned as he handed Prince Dave a strange new map.

"This looks familiar and yet so different! It can't be the map of the same mystical land we are now standing on, can it?" Dave asked, puzzled.

"But it is, my young prince! *Phantasy* is no longer just an ancient fantasy world shrouded in mystery anymore. It has been incorporated with electricity and modern technology ever since King Devonus discovered by accident the means to travel to the outside world when he was about your age, slightly younger though, I think."

"As you must have known by now, your Highness," continued Musscus, "the mighty fortified and self-sustaining palace was strategically built in the middle of the kingdom. We have tall towers on all four corners of the palace where our royal guards can keep an eye out for any abnormality or approaching enemies and trust me, young Prince Dave, we do have many potently dangerous adversaries you know nothing about! They don't just attack from the ground, they do attack from the air too you know. And sometimes even from the ground beneath! I shudder to think what will happen to us all and the king should the invisible force field weakens and disappear one day," Musscus was starting to pant now. In his excitement, he had spoken too much at one time.

Our young hero could not believe his ears as he absorbed all that his faithful bodyguard and friend had just said. This was the first time Prince Dave had seen Musscus said so much and he was even starting to pant like a normal four-legged canine which Dave had never seen him do before since they first met.

"Okay... Let me get me this straight," Dave said in a matter-of-fact way.

"So the royal palace is powered by electricity these days and I bet it's powered by a huge generator or two hidden somewhere within the palace grounds. And if there's electricity and modern technology even here in this modern improvised fantasy kingdom then that must also mean there must be modern conveniences such as air-conditioners, modern facilities and recreation centers, am I not right?" now it was Dave's turn to get excited at the prospect of visiting modern inventions surrounded by mystical history and creatures.

"Err, yes, your Highness, that is true," it was Hootus's turn to speak.

"Say, can you two show me where the nearest shopping mall is?" asked Dave as he stared with big innocent sweet eyes at Musscus and Hootus. "The weather is so hot today and I need to cool off."

"What?" Both Musscus and Hootus were kind of caught off-guard by this sudden request of their crown prince.

"Just kidding, guys!" laughed Dave. "You two should have seen the look on your faces, ha-ha-ha!"

And then in a more solemn tone, "Actually, I already knew about the modern technology that was incorporated into our kingdom from the other world. Dada told me about it not long after you guys brought me home. Besides, there're two air-cons in my bedroom and a few in Dada's. In fact, I believe just about every room in the palace has at least one!"

"Yes, of course there are shopping malls scattered here and there, your Highness," replied Hootus. "Only problem is, they are few and far and not easy to get to. Didn't you say you wanted to visit the more exotic and historical landmarks and places of interests in our magical kingdom in the first place? Besides, don't you get enough of those modern technologies back in the other world where they were discovered and invented, Sire?" Hootus asked, slightly baffled.

"Well..." Dave started to explain his current situation back in Singapore about how his financially-challenged foster parents couldn't afford much of anything in reality and all that but then thought the better of it. "Never mind, I'll tell you guys some other day."

"Yes. Yes, I guess I did," was the young prince's reply to Hootus's first question.

That was how our hero Prince Dave spent the last week of his June school vacation exploring the natural wonders of the magical kingdom of the Land of the Beyond which would one day be his, where nothing was impossible and the unimaginable waiting only to be discovered. There were indeed many strange and wonderful sights he did not regret visiting such as the few remaining defeated vassal states, scattered barbaric tribes and peaceful villages that surrendered and survived during the last war to unite the entire kingdom almost a thousand years ago. Dave had fun learning about their weird cultures and languages which, as was his young, restless and easily distracted nature he soon forgot about.

Then there were the many beautiful and picturesque works of nature such as the mountains, lakes, forests, caves, deserts, huge open grasslands, canyons, valleys, volcanoes and even mysterious craters of many different sizes scattered all over the kingdom nobody knew much of, except that they were ancient and had been there a long, long time. There were also the many farms that grew their own food and sold whatever they had no need for. Many had already begun modernizing themselves in order to catch up with the competition and times.

The young prince did have a great time exploring those places but there was one area he was told never to ever enter or even go near. It was a dark and forbidding corner of the kingdom known as the Dark Forest with a sinister history surrounded by a thick heavy black fog that never disappeared. Not even the great King Devonus himself dared step foot within that dark and creepy forest. He had been cautioned since young by his father who had been told countless horror stories about that creepy place by his father who had...well, you know.

All the time Dave was enjoying himself on his adventure as Dave the Explorer traversing the different parts of *Phantasy*, he was never able to get rid of the nagging feeling that he was secretly spied on. Musscus felt it too, of course. But every single time they turned around or turned in the direction where they thought they were being watched, there was never anything suspicious enough to hold their attention. Yet whatever it was that was spying on the teenaged prince would soon reveal itself and become his friend!

Watch out, Dave, a most deliciously evil danger is about to toy with you at the cost of your life!

(This concludes Chapter 15.)

CHAPTER 16:

SET A TRAP WE IS!

(Note: Just want to mention that this is my favorite chapter in this book and I've even dubbed it the "Classroom Scene". Even while working on this chapter I realized it has the characteristics of a Japanese manga! I love reading Japanese manga and watching Japanese anime! *Ichio,* **I wonder if this novel can be reworked into a manga and maybe even an anime someday. Dave-kun is such a** *'baka'* **and Snowpetal-chan is so** *'kawaii' neh***!)**

Monday, 30th of May, 1983. How time flew! The month-long June school holidays, it seemed, was over in the wink of an eye and school had, once again, commenced. Dave was back to being his lame old dreamy boring person nobody wanted to befriend. The good old days of being prince and living in a beautiful palace in another world that occurred not too long ago was now over and would not resume till the next month-long school vacation in December. The days of sheer torture and dreariness had barely begun and yet Dave was already wishing he was either dead or back permanently in *Phantasy*. Any amount of princely training (and treatment) was better than being the nobody that he was in school (and the 'real world') as well as being the constant target of fellow students and teachers alike!

However, subtle changes had already begun in young Dave's life which, no doubt, he would soon notice, no matter how hopelessly blur and slow he was.

It was the first day of school after the June school holidays had ended and class had barely started. Yet the whole class was already excited and buzzing with news but our hero could not be bothered what the fuss was all about and minded his own business sitting quietly in his corner day-dreaming as usual. The desks and chairs in every classroom in the secondary school Dave went to were arranged in such a way that every study desk and chair were in pairs and arranged neatly in rows and columns of fours by fives with the teacher's table seated solidly at the top left corner of the front of the classroom next to the chalkboard. Yes, chalkboard because the whiteboard, even though invented earlier, didn't really replace the chalkboard in classrooms all over the world until the 1990s. Good riddance to chalkboards and their cloudy dust!

It wasn't unusual for the seat next to Dave to be empty every single year that he attended that particular school. Who would want to be caught next to a born loser, especially *not* as his partner in class! Dave didn't mind at all though, for it meant nobody would be disturbing him other than the teacher while he was dreamily building castles in the air.

Unfortunately as it was for Dave, the next six months of that distinct year in school would be quite different for him and before he knew it, he would soon be the target of teasing of another kind he would never have expected.

Rumors had already been circulating in Upper Cross Secondary School even before school continued after the June school holiday had ended that a new and rich transfer student from a foreign land had enrolled in their school under rather unexpected and confidential circumstances. Sounds familiar? (Please refer back to Chapter 3 if you aren't.) Maybe but it's for very different and very wicked reasons this time around.

Not even the principal, Mr. Vincent Goh, knew much about the new transfer student, where she originated from or the reason for her abrupt change in environment. Except something about the exotic country where she came from was in some sort of political and military trouble and her rich and powerful parents had decided to send her to Singapore where it was relatively safe and their only precious daughter could continue with her studies in peace. Who hadn't heard of the wonderful education system in Singapore anyway?

What no one else knew about was how she had appeared ominously without warning as if by magic in the principal's house one day near the end of June with an official-looking letter demanding a place in his school into a particular classroom seated next to a particular student of his. And this strange new transfer student's name was? Just one word: Snowpetal. The principal, being the single, unmarried coward that he was in real life whose only hobby was to torture poor and helpless students with no means of resisting or fighting back (like Dave), was easily brain-washed into serving the young evil sorceress.

Mr. Vincent Goh; the principal of Upper Cross Secondary School, where Dave went to study as a teenager, became her latest pet and minion and now she had a place to stay in Singapore (for free some more wor!) while planning her next move. And boy, what luck! It was a posh condominium furnished with some of the latest and finest furniture and luxuries complete with some of the best facilities anyone can ask for that money can provide, situated in a secluded and affluent part of Singapore overlooking the vast and beautiful ocean, away from the usual bustling crowd. Frankly speaking, that was a bonus for hatching diabolical plans to deal with a live threat that was soon to exist no longer! Wait, how much did school principals earn anyway?

Dave's regular form tutor, Miss Jacinta Eleanor Fernandes, a very alluringly attractive young Indian-Eurasian woman with soft light brown skin and silky-smooth long dark brown hair, who never failed to capture the attention and fantasy of all her male counterparts wherever she went, had just stepped lightly into her classroom as if borne on wings, which was her usual charismatic style. All the male students in Dave's class immediately stood up and focused their attention on their comely form tutor, except for, well, Dave, who was dreamily staring out of his classroom windows waiting for the recess bell to sound, even though school had barely started for that day. Much to all the male students' and teachers' dismay in Dave's secondary school though, Miss Fernandes was already engaged to a young and handsome Indian pilot with a promising future who spoke perfect English, which was considered a very good catch in those days (unless one of the planes he flew crashed before he could get married, you never know, right?).

Soon, everybody in Dave's class stood up, including our main character, as he got poked in his fat ribs and bashed on his head for his attention as usual. Calling him by his name seldom worked as Dave was usually too deeply engrossed in his own fantasies to hear his name mentioned.

Miss Fernandes stared at her class with those huge sparkling brown almond shaped eyes of hers and after the same old boring class greetings proceeded to pleasantly announce that they had a new transfer student from somewhere unknown far away and invited her to step into the classroom to introduce herself.

"Huh, so it's a girl?" thought Dave. He had been paying attention despite his dreamy actions after all.

Snowpetal had grown bored outside the classroom whilst waiting for the stupid ugly teacher (in her own thoughts) to introduce her to her classroom so that she could start toying with her new prey ASAP. The petite and pretty yet murderously malicious sorceress with snow-white perfect skin and raven hair made her stood out from the rest of the crowd. Dressed in her new crisp school uniform with her hair tied into two pigtails that made her looked even more the part of an innocent fifteen year-old teenager, all heads and eyes were turned in Snowpetal's direction as she stepped quietly into her new classroom, even the girls' and yes, even Dave's.

Wolf whistles could be heard from the bolder and naughtier boys as Snowpetal introduced herself. Then her eyes searched and were fixed upon the cold empty seat next to Dave who was seated near the back of the class, a habit of his since his primary school days. This was a strategic move he made to ensure that he would not be so easily caught for not paying attention in class. A new and curiously odd sensation was dwelling up in Snowpetal's heart as she walked closer and closer to her target (yes, unlike her mentor and so-called 'uncle' she actually had a heart).

Dave, on the other hand, like and unlike the rest of the boys in his class at the same time, could not help but stared at the cute and pretty figure getting closer and closer to him. A new and strange feeling he had never felt before was rising in his heart as their eyes met for the very first time. Electricity seemed to appear and sparkle from out of nowhere between the two. Was this what people called true love? But how could this be? They had but met for only the first time and hardly knew each other. One was the soon-to-be savior of his world and the other was sent to ensure his demise. They could never be lovers let alone friends!

"Hi. Mind if I sit next to you?" Snowpetal's voice was soft and demure. No man could listen and say 'no' to such an angelic voice and form (imagine little angels with wings that look like Cupid, sans the bow and arrows, singing in harmony the moment one set his eyes on her). One look at her and it felt as if she was created directly from the hands of God Himself.

"Hi..." Dave parroted while staring dreamily at the most beautiful female form he had ever set his eyes upon (in his own opinion) standing shyly in front of him. "Hi and, err, sure...sure, why not..." Dave's voice trailed off as he continued staring and couldn't believe his luck (score, seriously, dude?). A new transfer student from some mysterious country had appeared in his school and now she was sitting next to him in class! Didn't know she would turn out to be this beautifully enchanting (and not to mention deliciously dangerous and maliciously evil as well!).

Snowpetal couldn't believe her luck either. This was going to be easier than she had initially expected. Her target was nothing more than a simpleton even though he was supposedly *the* prince of legend who would one day save his kingdom from her guardian and uncle who had taken care of her since she was a toddler.

The 'official' version of the story that Secondras had told Snowpetal as far back as she could remember was that her parents had been brutally murdered by merciless bandits cleverly disguised as travelling merchants who ambushed and raided their small state one night killing almost everybody, her parents included (that part was true, however...)! How Snowpetal had been miraculously saved the cruel fate suffered by her parents remained a mystery. All she knew was that she was found by her uncle Secondras as a baby after the raid had ended and the ruthless killers had left. She had been taken care of by him since then and she was eternally grateful for all that he had done for her. What Snowpetal never found out was the nefarious one responsible for leading the attack on her parents and their vassal state in the first place, until it was almost too late. Secondras wasn't her uncle. He never was and could never have been anybody's uncle to begin with!

"My, my...name's Dave. Dave Teo Chen Lee. You, you can, can call me Dave for short. What's yours?" giggles and laughter surrounded our love struck teenaged hero as he made a feeble attempt at introducing himself.

"Snowpetal. But you can call me Snow if you like," the strangely attractive new transfer student smiled shyly as she sat down next to Dave and had eyes for him only. Dave was happy and flattered such a beautiful girl was willing to sit next to him in class. In fact, it was the very first time any girl was sitting next to him out of their own free will! Maybe, just maybe they could become friends in the weeks to come. Who knew, right? If only Dave knew what her true intentions were, he would have avoided her at all costs!

There was something different about Snow's eyes that kept nagging at the back of Dave's head but he had no idea what it was. She smelled wonderful, looked great and was always there for him when he needed a helping hand or simply just a shoulder to cry on. Yet there was really something odd about Snow and it wasn't just her eyes. Nonetheless, the weeks and months passed by and as the evil young sorceress had planned, the doomed prince and never-to-be heir of his kingdom was eating right out her hands like the clueless fat yet cute puppy that he was.

Snowpetal had gained her victim's trust and now all that was on Dave's mind was the new transfer student herself who had become his closest best friend and they had grown inseparable. Dave even learned to ignore all the new endless cruel teasing from his peers and even teachers in school. He was used to being teased and bullied and this was nothing new. Maybe he had found his one and only true love after all.

Snowpetal continued her work in Singapore staying as close and often to her target as she could. She was slowly but surely gaining his trust and getting to know him better over the period they spent in school together. Snow reported to her boss whenever she could but over time, there was a gradual change in her and Secondras was a fool not to have noticed it.

Snowpetal was starting to spend more and more time in Singapore with Dave and less and less time with Secondras. Dave was, after all, the first boy she had ever truly encountered and got to know. Did Secondras take that into consideration before sending her out on this latest evil scheme of his? Even her reports were getting dull with little or nothing to report sometimes.

Could it be? A 'new' yet oddly familiar emotion was rising fast and furious within Secondras's black and shriveled heart by now. It was a new-old sensation for him which he had not felt for a truly long, long time now and when he did, all the pent-up ancient rage and frustration he had kept hidden from an era centuries ago came rushing back into his memories. That feeling Secondras wished he had truly forgotten since his childhood was none other than pure jealousy!

Be warned, Dave, and Snow too! A new and truly fierce and malevolent storm in all its raw gory form is now raging toward the two of you, and more!

(This concludes Chapter 16.)

CHAPTER 17:

THE LONG-AWAITED EPIC BATTLE.

The dawn of an end had finally arrived. The month-long year-end school holiday was just around the corner and things were not going very well for our young princely hero indeed. The nightmares had once again begun for Dave. Only this time, they were much more violent and horrifyingly graphic than before. Dave could even smell and taste the fetid stale blood and rotten flesh every single time after he had woken up and opened his tired and sleepy eyes from his all too realistic nightmares. But that wasn't his main concern, not that the nightmares bothered him anymore. They were only as irritating to him as the occasional mosquitoes hungry for his sweet delicious blood.

What truly worried and saddened him was the fact that he and Snow, whom he had come to fondly consider as his snow-mate, err, soul-mate by now, were seeing lesser and lesser of each other as the month-long December school holiday approached. As a matter of fact, Dave was already making plans for the two of them and was even hoping to bring her on a tour around his gigantic royal palace of a home back in the mystical modern fairy-tale kingdom when the school holiday started again (as if that was possible! Dream on, Dave.).

Alas, that was not meant to be! Snow's usual and only excuse? Her filthy-rich and forever busy businessman uncle, what else! He needed her assistance more than ever since the end of the year was just around the corner and business was picking up at a faster pace than before and it was more than he could cope with alone. Wasn't he married or something? Shouldn't his wife or at least, his own children be helping him instead of relying so much on his niece? Something smelled fishy here.

Snow explained to Dave that she couldn't say no to her uncle simply because he was her guardian and was more like both her parents put together since he was the one who brought her up when she became an orphan as a baby after both her parents were brutally murdered. Weekends and Sundays alike were 'family days' that her uncle had insisted (more like decreed) she *had* to spend with him and 'family members'. It was strange now that Dave thought about it. Snow never talked about her uncle and his own family and always avoided that topic as if it was taboo to talk about them, changing the subject even before Dave could ask her sometimes.

Even Dave's own father, who was king of a great mystical kingdom, was never this demanding! Nonetheless, Snow promised Dave that she would try to meet up with him whenever she could. Despite all her promises and reassurances, that didn't come true either, to Dave's disappointment. It sure was difficult to pass by each day without Snow's company even in school as the end of the school term for that year drew nearer and Dave tried his hardest to cope with it. But who was he kidding! He missed her badly and he felt there was something missing in his life whenever she was not by his side. Dave had the funny feeling her 'uncle' was selfishly keeping Snow by his side more than ever now on the pretext that his business was doing so well and that he was protecting her from (what, seriously?) the evils of the world (more likely from Dave himself).

Something didn't appear right, so thought Dave. On the one hand, Dave indeed felt really sorry for Snow. He felt really bad that Snow had lost her parents at such a young age and how she had no freedom to mingle and mix around with her friends after school and was more like a slave to her uncle. On the other hand though, she might have been lying to him all the while they were together just to gain his trust. But why would she do that? Unless Snow already knew about his true identity which Dave ruled out as totally impossible. Besides, she wouldn't hurt him at all now that they were already such close friends. Or would she?

Something just didn't feel right about Snow. Dave felt as if, as if, Snow was hiding something from him. While it was true they were now best of friends and all that, there were also many instances when they were together in school, Snow had tried to whisper into his ears something very important but every time she did, she would seemly stare into space, smiled sweetly at him and then continued where they had left off what they were previously doing, appearing like she was just being naughtily seductive and wasn't trying to tell him some secret or whatever it was she was trying to say.

Then there were the school rumors prior to Snow's sudden and unexpected appearance in Dave's school. So the school rumors about her parents sending her to Singapore to study weren't really true. It was her *uncle* who did it. Deep within his guts, Dave had this nagging feeling that Snow's uncle was actually trying to keep the two of them from spending too much time together. But how could that be? Dave didn't even know who Snow's uncle was so how could he have known about the two of them when they had kept to themselves all the time they were in school? Unless... First of all, her uncle was also here in Singapore, which seemed logical because she was often talking about him wanting her to spend more time with him, even during the weekends and how she hated that but had to comply nonetheless. Second thing was something Dave dreaded but was fast appearing as a possibility and that was that Snow had lied to him and was secretly reporting to her uncle their, or rather, his every move, which was the truth, actually. Still, Dave wished that wasn't the truth.

Another thing Dave had noticed was the new school janitor who appeared at the same time Snow did. Didn't Upper Cross Secondary School just employ a new janitor at the start of the new school term? Why the abrupt change in school janitors again? Was it a new school trend to keep changing the school janitor? Sure, that previous guy was young and lazy and didn't do his job half the time but still, Dave thought it was too harsh an action to have him fired and replaced with someone new so soon. Oh well, it wasn't Dave's problem to begin with and anyway, what's done couldn't be undone, right?

Still, there was something seriously weird about the new janitor. First of all, he was a big man. No, not very tall, he was more of an average height (around 1.70m). But he had really broad and muscular shoulders, a huge bulging chest and slightly protruding tummy. His entire body, it seemed, was covered with dark hair and he smelled like he hadn't bathed for months, maybe even years, who knew? Another noteworthy fact Dave noticed about the new janitor was that he never spoke, only grunting in acknowledgement once in a while, much like the sound an ape made, which really puzzled Dave a lot. Had the school's standard drop to such a low level that they had to hire somebody like that to be the school janitor? Was the school in some sort of financial trouble? Were they paying the new janitor with, what, bananas now instead of cold hard cash? What was next, Dave wondered.

By the way, Dave also noticed that he had not seen their school principal, Mr. Vincent Goh since school started after the June school holiday had concluded. Dave knew only too well that the middle-aged sadist would never miss school even for one day unless he was really, really sick or had meetings with the school's board of directors to attend elsewhere.

His reputation to torture hopelessly helpless students such as Dave himself was well-known in his own school and even to some extent, other schools. Besides, it was no secret their school principal was single and thus had no family of his own to keep him occupied at home. To be sick for a few days or even a week was a possibility even for someone as morally-challenged as Vincent Goh. But not to attend the school where he was in charge of for more than a few months now? Something really fishy was going on here and Dave smelled a big live one and intended to catch it, despite the fact that he was no fisherman!

Dave was genuinely worried for his school principal despite the way he had ill-treated him and many of his fellow students. Our kind-hearted teenaged hero had initially planned to visit his school principal at his home with his new best pal Snowpetal once the year-end school holiday had started. As usual though, Snow declined. Her uncle was now keeping an even tighter leash on her life after school and there was simply nothing she could do about it. Besides, Snow wasn't stupid enough to reveal to Dave that it was *her* who had cast a spell on their school principal in the first place that turned him into a mindless brain-chomping zombie and now, she was regretting it. So Dave decided to visit him on his own instead.

Ever since King Devonus paid a visit to Dave's foster parents at their rented 3-room flat in Chai Chee one evening, the Teos were more liberal with their foster son and his freedom. In fact, Dave would return home from school and not find his foster mother at home doing the housework and anxiously waiting for him to return from school as she used to.

It had become a habit that the Teos would both be home only late at night, just like the good old days. They refused to tell Dave anything despite his constant curious questioning, just that it was an 'adult thing' he wouldn't be able to comprehend as a child. So it ended up with Musscus always accompanying Dave home from school during the last six months in his canine form before the year-end school holiday begun in December, not that the young prince required it. Singapore was a safe country to live in really, even late at night, just as long as someone wasn't by himself or herself in a dark, secluded area, alone. Nevertheless, Musscus enjoyed the walk accompanying his teenaged crown prince home from school and it soon became their usual habit to chat as they strolled leisurely along the way. It was a ridiculously funny sight really to watch the two communicate with each other as they walked along. The one in school uniform would talk to his dog as if it understood and the other would bark back in reply as if it *actually* understood!

So Dave decided that he would one day drop by his school principal, Mr. Vincent Goh's posh condominium located somewhere in some quiet and wealthy neighborhood of Singapore, but only after taking the time and effort to find out his address, of course. And he would be escorted by his guard dog, Musscus, in the literal sense. The Dog-man was, by now, keeping a closer eye on his young royal master in both worlds, as a direct order from the king himself, and a gut feeling he had. As for Hootus, well, he was kind of playing house-keeper for the Teos at their rented 3-room flat in Chai Chee while they were away somewhere else, *elsewhere* (if you can catch my drift) in his human guise, which was, ironically, what he was trained for in the first place and one of his specialties. One can safely say Hootus was in the service line (lol).

Both Dave and Musscus were now standing outside Vincent Goh's private apartment. Since Musscus was a dog, he naturally started sniffing the air around them as he thought something was not quite right.

"Something's not right, your Highness," growled Musscus in a low voice, still in his canine form.

"I smell a strange rotten smell usually emanated from a corpse from behind this door, and it's moving! Also, there's this constant weird low moaning going on. Stand back, I'll try to break the door open and find out what's the decay is all about!"

"Wait, Musscus!" Dave stopped his faithful bodyguard as Musscus began his transformation from his dog form to his humanoid form. "There should be a security camera or two here on the ceiling if I'm not wrong. We have to enter by some other means."

Musscus was clearly impressed by his young master. Prince Dave had grown smarter and stronger within such a short duration that it was hard not to have noted the change in him. Musscus could see that his prince was finally maturing into the fine leader he was destined to become and hoped he would remain in their kingdom after the evil warlock had been vanquished forever and take over from King Devonus as the next great ruler of *Phantasy* as was the tradition when the time had come for his crown prince to do so. Until then, what were they getting themselves into?!

"What do you suggest then, my Lordship?" inquired Musscus expectantly. He didn't like the situation they were in currently but at the same time understood this was one of those predicaments that might help his prince grow up faster and teach him a thing or two about real-life encounters and how to cope with them. If he was not mistaken, there was indeed a zombie, a living and walking flesh-eating corpse behind that door and clearly the work of that nefarious warlock again. What Musscus wasn't able to figure out though was why the school principal and what had he done to offend the warlock? There didn't seem to be a link between the two at all. Or was there? How would the warlock benefit from the killing of his prince's mortal school principal? Or was it simply just a random careless act done out of boredom as the evil warlock was infamously known for?

"Well, there's always the *other* way to get around things when normal methods don't apply," Dave winked at his fellow companion and bodyguard. Now Musscus was all the more curious at what was cooking in his prince's head.

"Let me see if I can remember a spell or two that will get us into the apartment and find out what happened to my school principal, shall we?" Dave scratched his head as he tried to recall what few spells he had mastered and could remember at all during his training in his modern-day fairy-tale upgraded and updated kingdom many months back. "Oh, and let's move to the safety of the stairs before anybody finds us acting suspicious out here!"

Musscus nodded in agreement and before he knew it, they were now inside the principal's posh condo apartment...or what was once a posh condo unit that was now trashed beyond recognition and filled with blood stains all over the walls and expensive Italian marble floor. The entire place reeked of death and decay. Where was the principal? How could he even live in such filthy and smelly conditions? Wait, what was that creature that had turned its attention on them and was now shuffling toward them and moaning as if in pain? Although Dave had never encountered a real 'live' zombie before, he had heard, read and seen enough pictures of them to know how they behaved and looked like. And now here in front of him and Musscus was a real walking undead of a corpse smelling worse than his new school janitor!

Dave continued to stare incredulously (more like stunned speechless!) at the zombie shuffling awkwardly and slowly toward him and his bodyguard on its half-eaten twisted legs as it moaned softly, when he gradually recognized the balding head, distinct facial features, body shape and tattered clothes and realized who the zombie had been while it was still alive. It was none other than Vincent Goh, his school principal (yeah, right, what took you so long, dumbass)! No, wait, it was more like his *ex*-school principal, judging by the current situation.

"Watch out, your Majesty!" shouted Musscus as he pushed a stunned Prince Dave behind him and shielded him from the oncoming threat that was once human and Dave's school principal. With a few quick stokes of his gleaming double-handed sword Zepphire, the undead menace was no more with its head cleanly sliced from its body, the only certified and proper way to kill a zombie. A melancholy and nauseating feeling was rising from the pits of Dave's stomach to his mouth as the head of his former school principal rolled to a stop at his feet, mouth agape and all. Who was so cruel as to turn his school principal into an undead and why? Dave never found out, not that it mattered really.

Not much effort and time was required to clean up the mess in Vincent Goh's condominium, getting rid of the zombie remains and offensive smell and restoring his private apartment to its former posh glory, not especially with the help of a little magic here and there. Well, was there ever anything about the discovery of a zombie's remains hitting the headlines in Singapore's major newspapers in the 80s? No, right?

With the zombie episode behind and forgotten, Dave's only concern now was Snowpetal as he missed her very, very much. She was all he could think of. As it was back in the early 80s the mobile phone back then was few, limited and bulky as dinosaurs. Hardly anybody carried them then, only the rich and influential could afford to show them off. Since Snowpetal was a new foreigner in Singapore, she didn't have a local number Dave could contact her with at all. The same could be said for the computer and internet. Whatever we take for granted now wasn't easily available and affordable during that era.

Dave had become a truly love-struck teenager with no mood for anything at all now that his adorable companion had disappeared without a trace. All he did was hide in his tiny bedroom back in Chai Chee. Nothing his foster parents or even kingly father said or did could draw him out of his room, except during meal times. Everybody's got to eat no matter the circumstances, right? Everyone was worried sick for our teenaged love-struck listless hero. But sadly, nobody could do anything about it. Only time could heal the love-stricken youth now, or Snow's presence, a feasible but not very good idea though. Although Secondras's latest ploy hadn't exactly gone the way he had planned, it had worked nonetheless. Now was the best time to strike, whilst the iron was still hot!

Secondras the evil Warlock was the only one who knew his nemesis Prince Davy Fea Cotuus, eleventh generation of the Fea Cotuus legacy of *Phantasy*, should never ever reach his sixteenth birthday, or he would become too powerful even for the immortal warlock to defeat! If Dave did indeed managed to survive after turning sixteen, he would inherit the ancient powers of his kingdom and become what was known as a **Super Shenxien**, so proclaimed the ancient scrolls of history Secondras had managed to savage from some of the ancient ruins long, long ago.

Legend has it that one day a foreigner from another world that was a stranger to the Land of the Beyond, and yet not so, would appear in the kingdom's greatest time of need. He was the chosen child of the Land and be fooled not by his appearance for it deceives. Once the chosen child has returned to the land he was born from past sixteen years of age, rightfully inherit the ancient powers of his kingdom would he and become a force potent enough to be reckoned with. Defeat all evils that plagued his kingdom he will, especially the nefarious warlock who feared him the most and become a hero of his time he shall! Though soon to be forgotten by his own people be but part of his destiny. The **Super Shenxien** *be what that chosen child becomes. The last day of ever pending doom when the* **Super Shenxien** *finally come forth and saves the day!*

All of Secondras predictions had come true so far. Dave's sixteenth birthday was fast approaching and there was no better time than now for Secondras to strike now that the young prince had been reduced to nothing more than a useless love-struck teenager with no will to fight. And he knew there was no better candidate to end Dave's life than his one true love, Snowpetal! Oh, they would have made such a lovely cute little couple if they were allowed to live. But no, of course not and the vengeful and very jealous warlock would see to it that they both perished!

In a forgotten corner of *Phantasy* where the sun couldn't shine through and the moon avoided at all cost, clouded for an eternity by a mysterious thick black fog, laid a dark, dark forest known only as the Dark Forest. Deep, deep beneath that dark forest floor where no mere mortal dared venture was Secondras the nefarious Warlock's super-secret hidden evil lair. It was the one place where he preferred to spend most of his time planning evil schemes and his biggest fiendishly diabolical plot of all was about to become a reality! MUAHAHAHA!!!

The time to launch a full assault against the royal palace had arrived! And while everybody else was busy defending that no-good piece of reinforced stone and magic the king and his disgustingly goody loyal minions called home, Snowpetal would be able to end his nemesis's life with a knife through his heart with ease! None would be the wiser and Secondras would finally have his revenge and conquer the entire kingdom of *Phantasy* at the same time!!! What a brilliant plan it was, killing 3 birds with one stone! It was a pity though the young pretty sorceress he had groomed to be a wielder of sorcery since the age of three and come to grow so fondly of had to die. But then again that was the price she and everyone else had to pay for betraying him!

Monday, 19th of December, 1983. That was the day in the modern history of *Phantasy* that few of its inhabitants would forget. It was the day chaos and havoc reigned supreme. It was the day King Devonus had feared would come. And it had arrived slightly earlier than he had expected. Secondras had finally made his move. But the wise and aging king was already prepared. His only wish though was that if only his son was able to join him in the final epic battle for peace, not pieces.

The sky had turned a dark shade of grey in the morning of that fateful day, as if a storm was imminent. That was the first sign that trouble was brewing but most of the common simple folks of the magical kingdom failed to notice the significance of the change. They thought a normal storm was approaching. A storm was advancing for sure but it was no ordinary storm. It was a malevolent storm made of the vilest and nastiest creatures anyone has seen before. They came from all directions in all sizes and shapes imaginable. Some ran, some crawled, some rolled, some barrowed, some slithered and others flew. Their target? The fortified royal palace of *Phantasy* which stood tall and proud and mighty right smack in the middle of the kingdom itself of course, what else?

The palace was well stocked and prepared with all sorts of medieval weapons on standby for attacks of such enormous scales. There were the usual bowers with their arrows, catapults, boiling cauldrons of hot oil, and also some of latest tech warfare equipment (from the 80s) such as land-to-air missile launchers, heavy firearms and bombs. How King Devonus was actually able to acquire such modern weapons of mass destruction, nobody knew for sure. It was one of his secrets he wouldn't reveal. As for the invisible magical force field, let's just say King Devonus had gravely underestimated his arch nemesis.

After three days of continuous conflict, it appeared neither side was winning, or losing. But both sides had suffered heavy casualties. Yet neither was giving up the fight and throwing in the towel. The remaining forces had started slowing down and they were clearly exhausted. The area that surrounded the palace was now nothing more than blackened rubble. Bloody body parts were strewn everywhere and smoke and small fires were now a common sight. Screaming could still be heard from the hurt. It was a scene to be behold and nary for the fainthearted.

Even Secondras was spent as the weariness from all that fighting and killing was now visibly shown on his wrinkled twisted dark ancient face. Yet he was all smiles for he had won and conquered the land he stood on and had long desired to rule over, or so he thought. King Devonus's heart, he could feel and hear, was beating feebly which meant he had almost given up hope now. Even after three days of constant fighting, his one and only prodigy and hope, had not turned up to join his father by his side as the king had so wished.

Riding high and mighty on the back of his black undead dragon, Drakbane, Secondras the triumphant Warlock issued a final challenge to King Devonus just outside the broken gates of his dilapidated and divided palace that was once such a magnificent sight to behold. As the dust settled and smoke cleared, not one, not two, not three or even four but, well, quite a number of brave figures stood facing the evil warlock.

Secondras was slightly surprised but was he worried? The only one he truly feared had not shown his face even in this final grim hour that meant the fall of his father, king and ruler of a mighty kingdom that would soon be released from his hands permanently and with him, the proud legacy that had survived for almost a millennium now. And it was to fall at *his* hands, bloody as they already were with the blood of the countless innocent he had so enjoyed slaying over the centuries.

Standing at the frontline in all their full shining combat armor and glory were all seven members of the Seven Secret Elite Guardians of *Phantasy*, or S.S.E.G.P for short, with their weapons drawn and ready on the offense and Musscus as their leader. So they had decided to show their faces at last! Behind them were...what?!! What a surprise, Michael and Michelle Teo plus five uncles and one auntie of his presumably dead nemesis! Secondras certainly hadn't expected this. So the Teos had indeed ganged up with his arch nemesis, King Devonus and were secretly training hard all this time in martial arts in preparation for this final epic battle, eh? No matter, thought the malicious warlock, even their combined physical capabilities was still nothing compared to his hundreds of years of evil sorcery!

And of course, last and least of all, was the coward of a king himself hiding behind his so-called protective walls of loyal defenders who were most willing to sacrifice their lives for his without question!

"Well, well, well, this is all quite unexpected," mused the devilishly cunning and ancient warlock in all his gleaming splendor and flowing rich silk robes as he stepped off the back of his undead dragon mount and walked with calculated steps toward his 'welcome committee' as if it was a walk in the park.

"I was expecting a welcoming committee to welcome me as your new king but isn't this a bit too much?" said Secondras with both his arms outstretched as if he was welcoming his well, 'welcome committee'. He eyed all sixteen figures standing in their offensive stance, ready to strike at the slightest false move from the nefarious warlock, with an amused expression on his aged and wrinkled face which belied the truly dark and immoral being that Secondras really was.

"We can do this the easy way, or we can do this the easy way, for moi, that is!" a truly evil laughter escaped from the warlock's crooked mouth with all his rotten and black teeth on display as a dust storm suddenly erupted from out of nowhere and blew directly into the 16 heroes sending them reeling back in disarray, confused and lost.

Secondras muttered a spell and once again his appearance began to alter, he was expanding both horizontally and vertically, more vertically though and his skin turned dark and scaly, rows after rows of deadly sharp fangs appeared in his mouth and a tail sprouted out of his almost non-existent behind. He was turning into...Godzilla??? So where's Ultra Man when you needed him most? Nah, just kidding!

But the truth wasn't really that far off either. Before Secondras could finish his transformation into whatever giantic monster he had in mind, a shout commanding the vile warlock to stop in his destructive path could be heard over the fighting and screaming in the background. Could it be? Had Dave finally returned to his senses and was now ready to face the evil he and he alone was destined to overcome and destroy? Yes. Yes he was, from the look of his fresh and determined face as he stood holding hands with his lovely companion, Snowpetal. It seemed Dave had just awoken from a deep slumber not too long ago and was now fresh as a daisy and ready to face his most challenging challenge yet.

"Oh ho-ho! Look what the wind has brought us this time, another worthless life for me to snub out. Ah, there you are, my dearest Snowpetal! Shouldn't you be at *my* side holding *my* hand instead of the enemy's?" Secondras was sneering and so full of himself.

"No! Not after finding out the truth about my parents and how you cruelly murdered them in cold blood and took over their land and properties and me! You have deceived me long enough and don't ever expect me to return to your side, you dirty, filthy, perverted lying sadist for an excuse of an old man, you!" cried Snow as tears streamed down her pretty little fair face.

"So, took you long enough to find out, my little cute betrayer! No matter, you shall ALL perish RIGHT HERE, RIGHT NOW!!!" screamed Secondras the wicked Warlock as he lifted his wand and lighting appeared from the black sky and struck Snowpetal squarely in her chest. She collapsed where she stood and blood was already tickling from the side of her petal-shaped mouth. Smoke was rising from the spot where the single lighting had struck and there was a gaping hole near where Snow's heart was still beating. It seemed the warlock had missed his intended target. A simple "Oops!" was all that escaped from Secondras's mouth as he realized what he had done. He had wanted Snowpetal to die a fast and painless death. After all, she had done much for him and had served him well (in what manner I wonder) while she was still his apprentice. He had truly grown quite fond of her. Nonetheless, Snow was dying before Dave's eyes and he couldn't believe Secondras was really that cruel as the rumors had made him out to be.

"NO!!!" cried Prince Dave as he witnessed the life slowly ebbing out of his one true love, his soul-mate. "Please don't die, my snow princess...this can't be happening! We just got to know each other and I so want to spend more time with you! To get to know you better and more! Please, DON'T DIE!!! Not now, not yet!"

The young and furious crown prince of *Phantasy* then turned his attention to the one responsible for such a heinous misdeed, his eyes seriously burning with hatred, literally.

"MUAHAHAHA! See what I just did there?" boasted the nefarious warlock as he pointed a bony finger at the dying Snowpetal, who was really the princess of a small state by birthright that Secondras had stolen from her as well as the lives of her parents in just one night.

"That's the fate of all those who has betrayed me as well as those who goes against I! You have no idea what you are dealing with! I am Secondras, mighty immortal warlock and second to none! Bow before me as your new master and ruler of this kingdom and I may just consider sparing your puny little worthless lives!" Secondras looked exactly like the truly deliriously mad man that he was as he laughed most maliciously at the young prince, his father and the rest of his comrades. Maybe the power had gotten to his head such that there was no hope of any redemption left for him. Too bad.

"Not before I can do something about it!" It was a familiar yet totally different voice that came out of our hero Prince Dave as he slowly stood up and faced his nemesis for the last time. But not before he kissed Snowpetal tenderly on her cold cheeks and whispered softly into her ears not to die and wait for him to return.

Not only was there a look of pure determination on Dave's face, his eyes had changed from his usual dark brown to a bright sunny yellow. His entire body was also starting to glow and sparkle with electricity. Dave was growing stronger with every second passed as the fat on his body was miraculously replaced by solid muscles. But most incredible of all was the fact that blood was actually flowing out of Dave's scalp into his hair turning it stiffly upright and a bright crimson red in color. Was this the legendary **Super Shenxien** in question? Only Secondras knew but even in the last moments of his miserable life he was not saying anything, only trembling with fright as he stared at the completely transformed and impossible glowing form staring back at him.

To Musscus and Hootus, this form of their prince reminded them of the incident in the ancient ruins beneath their palace and that other instance outside the palace. Yet this time Prince Dave looked and felt even more different. It was as if, as if...the transformation was complete this time! So all it took to draw out the real Dave was anger and sorrow and seeing his loved ones hurt by evil? It was that simple yet hard to comprehend! This was beyond science and magic, beyond logic even yet it had happened before their very eyes! Prince Dave had become a legend, their kingdom's true hero after all!

"So the myth is real after all!" exclaimed a proud King Devonus. "My son is the legendary warrior of this kingdom who will appear in the face of true danger. The **Super Shenxien**. And now he has!" the king was laughing by now. His arch nemesis had heard what the king said and he was more afraid now than before! But Secondras was still showing no signs of fear. He knew if he did, his end would come even sooner! And he would fight with all his black magic and trickery to cheat death again. If he had cheated it once before he would cheat it again, simple as that!

"Enough!" screamed **Super Shenxien** Dave. "Your days of mayhem are over, Secondras you evil warlock! I'll make sure everyone sleeps in peace tonight and not have to worry about your vile presence again from tomorrow onward! Oh, and Dada, please do help me take of Snowpetal before I return after taking care of our nemesis here!" Prince Dave said as he winked at his father King Devonus before actually rising to the sky in a blast of hot air.

"Oh my," thought Devonus as he watched his son take off to the sky after the fleeing Secondras who had wasted no time taking to the sky on Drakbane, his trusty undead dragon mount even before the **Super Shenxien** had finished speaking. "He really does take after his old man, doesn't he?" the king said aloud, rather absentmindedly as he and everyone else watched the two figures in the sky getting smaller the further away they flew until they were no more than tiny specks in the dark gloomy sky.

It wasn't long before a fiery loud explosion followed by another and several others could be heard and seen in the distant sky. Had our hero succeeded in annihilating their accursed enemy? They could only wait in anticipation to find out.

About an hour had passed and there was still no sign of Prince Dave the **Super Shenxien**. What was going on? Had our young and inexperienced hero lost to the warlock after all? Had Secondras proven himself to be the superior of the two with his hundreds of years' worth of accumulated dark sorcery and tricks up his sleeves? Prince Dave, even with the ancient powers of the land he had inherited from, was still nothing more than a mere teenaged boy with little or no combat experience other than his three weeks of training during the June school holiday compared to the ancient wicked warlock with all his centuries worth of cunning and black magic. Had the darkest moment in the history of *Phantasy* actually come true?

Just when everybody had given up hope a blast of air appeared from out of nowhere and before anybody knew what had happened, a familiar figure stood before them after the dust had settled.

"I'm back as promised!" Prince Dave was coughing from all the dirt and dust he had created. "And I have also brought back a present for you guys," our hero proudly announced as he held up a bloody and twisted shriveled head for all to see, "as proof that the evil warlock we all hate and fear is no more!"

"Wait, don't believe him! That's not me! I would never do such a cruel thing as to remove the head of my enemy from his body! Not even from someone as evil as Secondras!" another voice very similar to Dave's said from the background.

What? There were now two Prince Dave??? Which was the real deal? Obviously Secondras had disguised himself as the teenaged hero as a last resort to save his sorry old hide.

"Sorry I'm late. I tried to catch up to the old fox but he sent his minions to block my path after narrowly escaping from me," the second Dave explained while panting slightly. It seemed his powers were wearing off. So there was a limit to his transformation.

"No, *I'm* your real Prince Dave!" cried the first Dave as he pointed to himself desperately. "He's the imposter! That's really

Secondras the truly infamous and powerful Warlock in disguise! Kill him while he's still weak and recovering his strength!!!" the first Dave was screaming hysterically by now, which was so unlike the usually quiet and shy Dave everybody knew. The other Dave could only look on, stunned at the unruly behavior of the first Dave. Had he ever behaved in such a way he wondered.

Musscus and Hootus gave their king a knowing look and they all nodded in unison. Suddenly all seventeen heroes, including Hootus, started charging at the first Dave together and gave him their all, obviously enjoying themselves as they beat the crap out of the defeated warlock they knew and hated so well. By the time everybody had stopped, the broken man lying before them had changed back to his real form, thoroughly reduced to a mere shadow of the powerful warlock that he had been moments earlier, hurt in more ways than one and truly defeated by now but still breathing nonetheless. Hey, good guys don't really kill, only as a last necessary means of self-defense, aye.

To ensure that the vanquished warlock could do no more harm, the main source of his corrupted powers was taken away from him, broken in half and buried deep beneath the royal palace, locked away in a magically sealed chest forever, along with his magic rings and other magical accessories.

As for the warlock himself, no, he was not beheaded nor executed in any way as everyone had hoped to be his fate. King Devonus argued and even pleaded with his son that that should be the correct way as far as tradition went. But Prince Dave, being the young and kind-hearted boy that he was, stubbornly refused to hear any of that bullshit, spared the ancient warlock's miserable life despite all the mayhem and destruction he had caused at the expense of numerous innocent lives.

Instead, Secondras the evil Warlock was locked away in the deepest and darkest dungeons of the Land of the Beyond to die a natural death of old age. To be lost in his own world and forgotten by all as time went by. After all, what fun was there in killing him and ending the tale now, especially, when the story from which Book 2: Oblivion - Land of the Forgotten, continued many years later after Book 1 had concluded, involving him and a few familiar faces as well as a new and darker terror?

What about Snowpetal, the dying princess? What about her? Oh, that's right! Everybody was so focused on the evil warlock they had forgotten about the pretty dying sorceress princess as she laid cold and lifeless, well almost, on the solid dirty ground. Everybody, except one person, that is. He immediately rushed to her side after ensuring that the warlock had indeed been truly subdued and was powerless to cause any more harm. By this time, Dave had returned to his normal chubby weak loser self.

As she lay dying in his arms, body turning cold and hard, Snowpetal looked into Dave's eyes and there appeared many questions in her head she had wanted to ask him. But time was running out fast. As her petal-shaped rose-red lips parted to say something, Dave kissed Snow lightly on her sensual lips to hush her.

"Do you know what this is, my dearest?" tears were unconsciously rolling down his fat cheeks as our young hero placed one hand in front of Snowpetal's beautiful pale white face whilst staring intently at her and holding one of her cold hands firmly with his other free hand.

More blood tickled down the side of Snow's mouth as she laughed and coughed at the same time. "Don't be silly, Dave!" she smiled faintly. "That's your big, fat and ugly hand of course!" Snow's voice was almost inaudible as she feebly said those words in a teasing tone.

"No, it's not, you silly girl!" Dave begged to differ.

"What you see here is not merely just my hand. This is *the* hand that will protect you and keep you warm with a fuzzy feeling within your heart for the rest of your life, my dearest. I promise you that for as long as I live and breathe!" Dave proclaimed with the most solemn look on his face he could muster as he tried his hardest not to shed any more tears in front of Snowpetal as he held her white soft and freezing cold hands in his.

"No, you silly little prince, you! That will never happen!" exclaimed Snow weakly as her life-force and color continued to drain from her almost lifeless cold body.

"I...I'm so, so cold, Dave. So, so very cold. Hold me tighter, will you? Don't let me go, please!" pleaded Snowpetal as a genuine look of fear appeared in her eyes. "I'm so cold...and frightened, Dave. They are coming for me! Stay with me, Dave, stay with me please..."

"NOOOOO!!!" cried a truly heart-broken Dave as he hugged the totally cold and motionless body of the (once evil) snow sorceress princess tightly never ever letting her go, even in death. He had so much planned for them. They were so going to get to know each other better in the near future, fall deeply in love, marry, have many wonderful children together, live and grow old and maybe even die together, just like in the many magical fairy-tales he had read when he was younger. Why couldn't *his* fairy-tale have a happy ending like so many others too!

It was too late. Prince Dave could only watch helplessly as Snowpetal's body continued to crystallize and break into tiny shiny fragments. That was too much for our young broken-hearted hero to bear. The one true and only friend he had ever known in his short young life was now gone forever. Truly gone and never ever coming back to haunt, I mean, taunt and seek his company again. They were like two lost souls in an equally cruel and heartless world. What was he to do now that his soul-mate was gone forever? There wasn't even a body he could remember by. Was she that evil before they met? But of course it wasn't her fault she was that immoral, it was that vile warlock who turned her out that way by tricking her and making her his puppet and doing his dirty work for him! Dave started to regret letting Secondras carry on with his life but what's done was done.

Life seemed to have no meaning for Dave anymore as his mind went totally blank while he continued staring at the spot where his snow princess had just died. There remained not a tell-tale sign she was ever there as a strong gust of chilly wind blew away whatever remaining fragments of Snowpetal's body there was.

"I love you, Dave, and always will. I'm sorry for my past misdeeds. Goodbye, my love!..." a faint and ghostly familiar voice meant only for Dave's ears was whispered along with the wind that swept whatever remained of Snow's body away.

Prince Dave would have remained rooted to the spot had a strong arm not come along and pulled him to his feet.

"I'm sorry for your loss, son. Snap out of it, will you? It's over! We did it! The evil has been neutralized and it's time to celebrate. Besides, I'm sure there are a lot of other beautiful maidens out there for you, Dave! You will get over it in due time, son, don't worry," King Devonus sure was optimistic. But that was only on the surface as it was his way of trying to cheer his son up. Inside his heart though, he felt just as terrible as Dave did; bitter and lost.

"I'm not so sure, Dada," Dave's voice was low and almost quiet, as if lacking the energy to carry on. "I just wish to be left alone for now, please."

"Well, sure thing, son, sure," King Devonus wasn't exactly a stranger to the way his son felt. The king himself felt exactly the same way after his one and only wife Queen Katrina had died not long after giving birth to their son Prince Dave. And now he started to feel bad for his son too.

"By the way, just out of curiosity, what happened during the three days we were fighting for our lives? You didn't appear till the very last moment and we were all worried sick for you," King Devonus was worried for his son, being the caring and doting father that he was.

"Sorry, Dada, I'm really tired now. Tell you in the next chapter, ok? Err, I mean, next day, next day!"

King Devonus couldn't help but raised an eyebrow as he watched the listless and completely drained figure stumbled awkwardly back to the palace and into his own princely bedroom, which was already under repair even though the final epic battle was just over.

(This concludes Chapter 17.)

CHAPTER 18:

IS IT TRULY OVER?

Life, love, sickness...and finally death. In only the short span of...
*Oh wait! This looks like the starting of the epilogue, not the last
chapter! My bad! It seems I have misplaced the last chapter of my novel
with the epilogue in my haste to end it, ha-ha-ha... Let's do this all over
again, shall we?*

The atmosphere of the palace and its denizens were unusually
silent and somber the day after the epic battle of good versus
evil. There were no celebrations or parties throughout the entire
kingdom even though King Devonus had declared that day a public
holiday and its people were free to do as they pleased. It was still hard
to believe that tranquility had finally returned to their kingdom and
the eternal menace that had plagued them and their forbearers alike
had been put to a halt once and for all.

It seemed that the subjects of his mysteriously mystical
kingdom would rather spend their time rebuilding their kingdom
right after the epic battle that lasted for three solid days and nights
than celebrate. Besides, most of those who survived the fight were
exhausted, injured and in no mood to celebrate. The celebration,
they reasoned, could come after everything was rebuilt and their
lives back to normal.

It was way past noon by the time Prince Dave woke up. He had the strangest dream the night before. There was nothing evil about it really. He dreamt that his snow princess was now in another dimension together with her real parents and was happy to be reunited with them again. She had been given another chance to live once more given the circumstances that she was tricked into performing the nefarious warlock's evil deeds for him while she was under his care. Also taken into consideration was the fact that she was sober enough to switch sides at the last minute and joined Dave in the epic battle against her former master and so-called uncle.

In his dream, Dave was by her side as they used to be before Secondras intervened and separated them. She told him they would meet again but not until many years later in some other parts of the other world (hint-hint). Dave was confused by what she had said and that was when he woke up from his deep slumber, still sleepy and bewildered by the unearthly dream he had the night before.

As he had promised, our hero explained to his father what had transpired to him the three days he had been missing in action.

The last time anybody saw the teenaged prince before the epic battle; he was moping in his tiny bedroom back in Chai Chee, Singapore and was in such a disoriented state all because he missed his Snowpetal. When Secondras initiated his assault on King Devonus and his royal palace, Hootus was the only one left behind to babysit him since he knew nothing about fighting. Hootus was more the poet and lover, not a fighter!

While Dave was sleeping soundly one night in his tiny bedroom, he had a most curious dream. Two regal-looking visitors dressed as finely as his kingly father had come knocking on the door at his foster parents' Chai Chee flat and oddly enough, there was nobody else home that day save Dave himself. Dave politely greeted them and invited them in despite not knowing who they were. There was something queer about them that he found he could *relate* to and yet...

It wasn't until they formally introduced themselves that Dave finally realized who they were! They were his deceased (half-) uncle and (half-) auntie from his father's side! Wait, Dave was truly confounded by a few things after the two royal visitors had disclosed their identities and his head started spinning.

Wasn't his father King Devonus supposedly the *only* child in their lineage as was the tradition? The second thing was the creepiest part of all. How could they visit him if they were already dead!!! Oh, they explained to Dave that it was only a dream and in dreams, anything was possible! Right...?

Yes, while it was true there could only be officially one descendant of the royal lineage and it *had* to be male in order to carry on with the sovereign heritage. But there were also some very rare cases where the firstborn was female and thus given away to the...less regal such as the nobles and others of such distinguished status. Another possibility was if the king had some secret flings on the side and in the process some illegitimate prodigies were undoubtedly procreated and it didn't matter if they were male or female. After all, kings were men too, weren't they? Even kings (and queens too) had the right to mingle and fool around once in a while.

As for Dave's, or rather, his father King Devonus's case, it was the latter that unfortunately came about. His dead half-aunt was his father's half-sister, the outcome from one of his grandfather's secret rendezvous with a sexy duchess from a vassal state. His grandfather, King Otellus knew about her but could do nothing about it. The most he could do was to make sure she married someone of the same status as her or higher in order to secure a better life. It was all that King Otellus could do for her.

But that was not what the two royal ghosts had come to see their half-nephew about. They had come to warn him of an imminent danger. The only thing that could prevent his untimely death was this lovely bejeweled and expensive-looking sparkling gold chain necklace Dave *had* to present to his would-be assailant. If not...

Before they left, Dave's deceased half-aunt added that his would-be assassin was actually their daughter (come again?!) and someone he knew and liked very much indeed. What did they mean by that? Dave was befuddled as usual. He sure was getting a lot of weird dreams lately! The only girl he ever knew and like was...

Sure enough, just as he opened his eyes after he had woken up from his dream, there was Snowpetal staring right at his face - with a dagger in her hands ready to strike at his heart!!! Where was Hootus? Wasn't his personal butler supposed to look after him? Dave looked about him and there was Hootus, lying unconscious on the floor next to his mattress. He had been knocked out cold trying to stop her from killing his fragile prince. Luckily for our young hero, he remembered what his dead half-aunt had mentioned from seemingly moments earlier. With a nimble and swift swipe of his chubby hands, Dave placed the necklace that sparkled with a magical radiance which had miraculously and mysteriously appeared in his hands after he had woken up from his strange dream. Was it a dream at all or did his dead royal relatives actually pay him a visit while he was *half* asleep???!!!

Nonetheless, the sparkling necklace with its magical properties had done its part. The blank look disappeared from Snowpetal's eyes as she awoke from her trance-like state, and dropped the dagger she was holding, dangerously close to where Dave was lying on his mattress just moments earlier.

"Dave...? What are you doing here? Wait, where am I?" asked a disturbed and perplexed Snow as she looked around her unfamiliar surroundings.

Something better was yet to come. The magic in the necklace was not yet done. Snowpetal was truly stunned and surprised as the memories from within the magical regal heirloom flooded into Snow's pretty little head.

After ten minutes or so, tears started to flow freely from the snow princess's eyes as she found out the truth about her real parents and their murders as well as her true royal birth.

Dave was speechless as Snowpetal recounted to him what she had just seen in her mind. And also the fact that she had once worked for Secondras, of her own free will. If only she had found out he was the one responsible for her being an orphan sooner! Still, it was not too late, she hoped.

A single tear rolled down King Devonus's face after he had heard Dave's side of the story. If only he had known that Snowpetal was his missing half-niece earlier, he would have rushed to her side and blocked the lighting with his own shield from hitting her! Instead, he had watched with indifference from a safe distance while she was struck and dying from the evil warlock's misdeed. And now his heart was heavy with guilt. But it was too late. Snow was dead and gone forever and there was not even a body he could remember her by.

But there was something else even more mystifying that bothered the king. He had known about the legend of the **Super Shenxien** from his father who had known about it from his father who knew about it from... Anyway, didn't the ancient scroll state that the **Super Shenxien** would awaken only when the chosen one had turned sixteen and not sooner or later? The king was truly puzzled, until he pondered long and hard and suddenly remembered and realized something he had long forgotten!

The Teos had received his son on Christmas day itself! They could only assume he was born on that day since the king himself delivered Dave to their doorstep only on that fateful day. In reality, Prince Dave had been born a few days prior and the king had been too devastated about his wife's death to care about his son whom he had neglected and blamed his wife's, Dave's natural mother, Queen Katrina's death upon. Instead and indeed, when King Devonus thought about it, his son's birthday was, as a matter of fact, the third day of the epic battle! What a coincidence indeed! Fate had a funny way of setting things right, it seemed.

'*The last day of ever pending doom when the* **Super Shenxien** *finally come forth and saves the day!*'

That last sentence from the ancient scroll was what puzzled King Devonus the most and he finally understood what they meant! Now his only wish left was to hand over his kingdom to his son, Prince Dave once he had reached adulthood and the old king could finally retire in peace. Or so he thought.

(This concludes Chapter 18.)

Epilogue:

LIFE AFTER *PHANTASY.*

(Note: Whatever is stated here in the epilogue in Book 1 is strongly linked to Book 2 and Book 3. The events stated in this epilogue are a glimpse of what's in store for the next 2 books. After all, they are linked and part of a trilogy. Their appearances will however depend on you readers. You have been warned.)

Life, love, sickness...and finally death. In only the short span of a few months' time Dave had experienced all that life had to throw at him, and probably more than he had ever realized. Albeit only a mere teenager of fifteen with a short and rotund stature not many would ever consider giving a second look, Dave had gone from a nobody and a loser to a fine prince and mighty savior of his country, *Phantasy*; an ancient civilization still shrouded in mystery and fantasy today, even though it has been modernized, to a certain degree.

Seemingly, in the wink of an eye he had mustered the courage and strength to face and defeat a great and truly sick evil that had terrorized his people and country for ages. Dave also had his first ever taste of true love along the way...only to lose her in the hands of the sinfully immoral and wicked warlock he had no idea was truly the embodiment of pure evil (figuratively speaking)! Having rightfully earned the lion's share in stopping the power-crazy and vengeful Secondras (and let's not forget sparing his life as well) and his minions from causing anymore mischief and wreaking havoc for good (hopefully), Dave had done what his father, King Devonus, had not managed to do his entire life.

But has the prophecy been truly fulfilled? Or was there indeed more to it than meets the eye? Stay tuned to the next book to find out!

Under any normal circumstances, being a man, Devonus would have been filled with rage and jealousy by now. It was his son Prince Dave the **Super Shenxien** who did most of the work halting the great and immortal Secondras the (almost) indestructible Warlock, nary him or anybody else. Dave was the one granted credit in the downfall of their arch nemesis unanimously by everybody present in the epic battle, not the king of *Phantasy*, certainly not Devonus the king himself! But, of course, Devonus was no ordinary man. He was king of a great country and he had trained his whole life more than anyone else to put an end to his revenge-hungry and insane arch enemy.

Secretly though, unbeknownst to everyone else but the king himself, he had wished his 'long-lost' son to be there in the final hours to aid him when he was needed. Devonus had expected to save his only son from the warlock's wrath whilst they fought valiantly side by side during their epic battle against the ancient mad warlock. In other words, King Devonus so wanted to be the hero and center of attention and not his son (lol). It was a fantasy after all but hey, even a king can afford to day-dream once in a while, right?

Now what? With his arch nemesis finally out of the picture and his kingdom returning to the way things were before the nightmares began, there wasn't really much left for the king to do every day anymore. Most of the problems in his fairy-tale kingdom were caused by the warlock and his minions after all. He had lost his one and only true love Queen Katrina so spending time alone with his loved one was impossible, even for a magnificent king from a fairy-tale fantasy kingdom full of wonders and filled with magic. Age has started to catch up to him and to make matters worse, Devonus knew that one of his worst fears was coming true: he was going to lose his only heir to their great and extraordinary magical kingdom, again!

Both father and son might not have been as close as they wished they had and both of them might not have been reunited for long. But King Devonus had been through a lot himself and had seen very much of the different worlds and countries out there that existed. He knew well enough from his own experiences and the body language of his only son, Prince Dave, that Dave had no desire to stay and rule their kingdom together.

Devonus was now desperate and a new plan was starting to hatch in that wonderful yet unpredictable mind of his. He was getting old after all and needed a successor to his throne just as his father and grandfather and generations before them had done. It was a tradition that should NEVER be broken! For once broken, the kingdom known as *Phantasy*, the Land of the Beyond would cease to exist altogether as predicted. In other words, that would only mean that all that blood sacrificed and sweat lost by King Devonus and his ancestors into building this dream kingdom of theirs would have all been for naught! No, something HAD to be done indeed!!!

It was an unthinkable move and the aging king was at his wit's end. He was running out of options fast. Devonus had already tried his best convincing Dave into settling down in his home land for good after completing his studies in Singapore and living the kingly life that was his true destiny and ruling a whole kingdom that was his for as long as he lived. Oh, did Dave even realize how many ordinary folks out there would have killed him to be in his shoes! All that luxury and riches, for *life*! Not to mention the authority to order anybody he wished and the freedom to do as he pleased! (Just a gentler reminder here: Being king isn't exactly just all that mentioned above. There're also the responsibilities and duties a king has to perform and answer to his people, in the good ole days anyway. Not so sure about the modern monarch of our time though.)

Dave was indeed one of the luckiest people in the whole wide universe to have been born into royalty! It wasn't every day that a random baby gets born into royalty you know! Who would take good of the king in his old age? He couldn't simply transfer ownership of the entire kingdom to just any tom, dick or harry after he had gotten too old to rule! And the reasons in the list went on. Yet despite the king's best efforts, Dave was nevertheless adamant about leaving *Phantasy* for good and would rather live the life of a commoner in the other world! The young prince was as stubborn as he was vertically-challenged. (What? You thought I was going to say 'fat'?)

King Devonus had been entertaining this certain...ridiculously possible yet morally unjust thought for a while now. Perhaps there was a reason his arch nemesis was spared. Perhaps it was not such a bad idea to work with the enemy. After all, it could only benefit both parties in the end. Really? Was the king so desperate that he gone out of his mind?

A few months had passed since the defeat and capture of one of the greatest evil and madman the history of the fabled Land of the Beyond had ever known. His minions were sighted less and less often as the once hectic pace of life before the storm slowed to a norm and the present days proceeded lazily by again, especially in *Phantasy*, where it all started, and ended. Or has it?

It was decreed in the now peaceful and sleepy kingdom not long after his defeat that the evil warlock's name was never to be mentioned ever again! Anyone caught mentioning even the slightest hint of *his* name would not only have his private properties confiscated but his (or her) immediate family sent without further ado to the gallows! Such was the outcome and evil reputation that Secondras the nefarious Warlock had achieved! Even though powerless and left to rot deep in the dungeons, his reign of terror still ruled (hi five! Oh, no? Bad idea, eh?)!

Dave the Commoner Prince had grown quite accustomed to teleporting between worlds via magical means (not beans, okay?) and their various side effects by now. Most of the time he would end up at his intended destination, in one piece. Unfortunately enough there were those rare occasions whereby he ended up in places he never knew existed in the weirdest form unimaginable or parts of him replaced with...well, you get the idea.

The (mainly) countryside scenery in the Land of the Beyond was a nice refreshing change from the concrete jungle that was all Singapore. But none of that mattered to Dave at the moment. He didn't come back to enjoy the rustic terrain nor visit anybody really. He had made up his mind and he was back one last time in the land he was born in to bid a final farewell to family and maybe all the new acquaintances and friendships he had forged on his journey to destroy the pure evil that was his destiny as crown prince of his kingdom.

"You're finally here, son!" King Devonus was all smiles as he welcomed and greeted his son, Prince Dave, not suspecting that that was the last time they would meet (until the next book, that is).

"Wait, stop! Dada, I, I'm came back only to tell you something. I'm not here for the party, sorry."

Dave took a deep breath and settled himself before speaking his mind, "I know you love me and all that, Dada dearest (oh-oh). But really, you can't force me to stay and rule by your side till I'm old enough to run this kingdom on my own! Besides", Dave continued as he went closer to the father he wished he had known all his life and was never parted from by a cruel twist of fate, "you will always be my only Dada no matter what and I'll always, always love you and remember you for who you are and what you are."

"No one, and I mean, *no one,* can absolutely ever replace you as my father and Sire," said a teary Dave as he placed a fat hand on Devonus's shoulder. "Not even my foster parents who have brought me up and taken care of and protected me all these sixteen years of my life."

Tears were quietly running down King Devonus's face as he absorbed what his son had just said to him. He really wanted to stop his only son and heir to his kingdom from leaving, very very much. But what Dave said next put a total stop to whatever scheme Devonus had planned inside his head to prevent his son from leaving *Phantasy* forever.

"Frankly speaking, Dada, there are more sad memories here than happy ones for me. I'm not the bold and adventurous type of person who enjoys fighting and going on adventures all the time! You know that and you know very well what I'd prefer to do with my life. I'm...nothing like you! We don't even look alike! Who will believe us if we tell them we are father and son, sharing the same family tree and even coming from a long line of kings?"

"And then, and then there's...Snow," the tears were pouring more viciously down Dave's fat cheeks as he mentioned the dead snow princess's name.

"She may have done a lot of bad things in the past but it wasn't exactly her fault! She was misguided at a very young tender age! She may have been a lot of nasty things to you but she was true to me and now she's gone forever and will never come back to me and spend the rest of her life with me ever!"

At the mention of the snow princess's name, guilt once again filled King Devonus's heart. There was something he had kept from his son since the epic battle of good verus evil. Musscus had reported to him the two instances of Dave's transformations prior to the final encounter with the warlock, both of which were short and full of faults. After a lot time spent considering all the factors leading up to Dave's physical changes and studying them from different angles, the king finally came to a conclusion which he told no one, not even to the duo he trusted most.

If only he had told someone, especially his best royal guard and leader of the S.S.E.G.P, maybe Snowpetal would have been alive and well today and Dave might not have disregarded his destiny as future king and ruler of *Phantasy*. The two might even have married and the hope for their doomed kingdom would have continued through the son of his son!

But then again, if Snow had been saved, Devonus feared that nothing else would be traumatic enough to trigger the ultimate transformation in Dave that would draw out their true savior, the **Super Shenxien,** defeat their common arch nemesis and save the entire kingdom from certain death. Without the **Super Shenxien,** there wouldn't even be a kingdom left to rule, let alone thoughts about the next generation of ruler after Dave!

The king thought he had done the right thing sacrificing one life for the rest of his people and kingdom. He would have done the noble deed of sacrificing himself, he had considered that option. But the fact that the crown prince was still young and wet behind the ears left him with no other alternatives. His subjects needed him still if they survived the fight against the evil warlock and his minions, which they had, with the help of the **Super Shenxien** who had been awakened, all thanks to Snowpetal and a little help from the nefarious warlock himself.

But that was all before the fact that the snow princess was actually his long-lost missing half-niece whom he had been searching for in vain was revealed to him. If only he had found out earlier. But it was too late and there was nothing he could do now. Perhaps it was not such a good idea to team up with the warlock after all, desperate for a heir as the aging king was. King Devonus took his latest setback as retribution. He had retained his nation but lost a son and heir to his throne in the process.

Dave ran teary eyed out of the throne room and far, far away from the fortified palace of *Phantasy*, vowing never to ever set foot back into that accursed kingdom again.

Dave tried his best to totally forget about that magical episode of his teenage years by studying hard. Unfortunately, school life also reminded him of the loss of the love of his life and all the wonderful time they had shared together. Dave quit school and studies altogether after he had graduated from Upper Cross Secondary School scoring moderately for his 'O' Levels. The teenager started working hard by joining the competitive rat race at the age of seventeen. Eventually the young man found a suitable job after years of job-hopping and was determined to stick with it. Dave never looked back since and neither did he regret leaving *Phantasy* and putting his royal life and magical past behind him for good.

Once again, that is another story for another day, little ones.
Lights out and sweet dreams!

THE END (1)

Just as he took in a deep breath and was about to retire for the night himself, the light on old Dave's personal intercom sparkled abruptly and came to life.

Something deep within Dave's guts told him this was nothing good. A dark and ominous storm of ruthless metallic origins was rising with increasingly precise and inhumane speed in the horizon.

A familiar young feminine voice could be heard over the uproar in the background that was struggling desperately to gain Dave's attention. Old man Dave hesitated slightly before pushing the 'talk' button.

"Yes, Flight Lieutenant General Aries, and how may I assist you this time?"

Loud static and then, "The situation has turned bad, real bad, General Dave, sir! You were correct after all. The robots on planet Zortron have all turn renegade as you have predicted and are planning an all-out attack against all humanity! They are already assaulting some of our more peaceful planets and anything of human origins in their way even as we speak, sir!"

Old Dave was literally staring into deep space as he thought hard and fast.

A part of Dave was putting in his best effort not to shout "I told you people so!" into the microphone just as another part of him remembered the countless number of times he had been ridiculed by the Universal Council of Inter-Space Alliance (U.C.I.S.A for short) over his so-called 'crazy' theories that the robots they have created in the past were now beginning to evolve at an alarming speed and had started to think and fend for themselves. They were even covertly planning to overthrow their masters, the humans. Some of those council members were even family and they too had turned away in shame to Dave's controversial and dubious theories.

Most of universal council members consisting of different alien species, mixed human races as well as the pure human ones originally from planet Earth had refused to listen to Dave's so-called 'crazy theories from an old man' as they either did not want to become involved with a problem their kind had not started or had simply thought that age had finally caught up with old man Dave and he was slowly turning senile. Dave was after all already one hundred and fifty years old and not as nimble and lively as he used to be. Old Dave could only resign to his fate for what little evidence he had in his possession had been rendered useless by the traitorous robots. Most of the incidents Dave had cited were dismissed as either 'pure coincidences' or 'isolated cases' that didn't occur on a frequent basis.

Instead, the great grandfather and once revered council member counted to ten and said in a calm voice, "It's alright, Aries. Forget about the formalities. What's your current location? Don't lose hope, okay? I'll be right there with KNITE as backup AFAP!"

"Oh, and Aries, I love you, remember that for you're my favourite granddaughter!"

"I know, grand Dada, I love you too!"

Crying, screaming and shouting could be heard before the intercom went dead and old man Dave feared for the worst.

"Damn you, Zortron! If only..." was all that was on Dave's mind as he hurried toward the hangar his trusty robot counterpart was housed in.

THE END (2)